FOREVER
SOULSISTERS

The Indigo Adventure

Heather & Samara Silverman

First published: 2016

First e-book edition: 2016

ISBN 978-0-692-63880-4

Library of Congress Control Number 2015908279

SoulSisters Forever, Inc.

www.foreversoulsisters.com

We dedicate this book to our parents, who supported and encouraged us to fulfill our dreams. We are eternally grateful.

CHAPTER ½

JAYCEE

We never really understood how we could be twin sisters. The Barron twins, that's how Alexa and I are commonly referred to around our town off Lollie Hills. If it weren't for that introduction, I don't think anyone would really think we were related. We're different in so many ways.

Alexa, but everyone calls her Lex, is quiet and mostly keeps to herself. She frequents the library on a daily basis, during lunch and after school.

I, on the other hand, prefer to be called Jay. I am a cheerleader and president of the sixth grade. I spend my free time browsing for cute boys and outfits at our local shopping mall.

Growing up, Alexa often asked me, "If we weren't sisters, do you think we would be friends?"

I always answered the same way: "No, definitely not."

Unbeknownst to us, it was our differences that brought us together, in a way that we never thought possible. One summer changed everything.

ALEXA

I couldn't believe that Grandma was here with us. I felt like I hadn't seen her in such a long time, and now here she was in the same room. She was still one of the most beautiful people I have ever seen. Her innate charm and charisma usually attracted a following, so it was of no surprise to me that a group of people were gathered around her. I wondered who they were. I didn't recall meeting any of them before. I stood next to Jay and looked back at Grandma.

Grandma was elegant as always. She wore a tailored white suit and a royal blue satin blouse. I was immediately mesmerized by her turquoise blue eyes and porcelain skin. Her red hair was curled and pulled back in a loose knot. She seemed more like an angel than our Grandma.

Grandma looked at us from the center of the theater-like room. It commanded a presence with its high ceilings and iridescent glow.

Behind Grandma there was a large mahogany table with ten tall, gold velvet chairs. We watched as everyone took a seat. Grandma put her index finger against her mouth, gesturing for us to keep quiet. We observed in silence and looked around the table, not believing our eyes.

Jay, Grandma, and I took up three of the seats. "How can this be? We are right here, how are we also there?" I asked Jay in disbelief. "It's like watching ourselves in a movie."

Seated in the fourth chair was a boy who looked so familiar to me. I thought hard. Who was he?

Jay let out a big gasp and whispered, "Lex, that's him, that's him."

JAYCEE

No way! Was it really him? How was he here in this room? I felt my heart skip a beat, and it started to ache a little, as I watched him seated so close to me.

His big blue eyes looked down at the paper. His curly blonde hair was messy on top of his head. I had forgotten how cute he was. The last time we were together I'd run away from him. I felt so bad. I bet he didn't like me anymore. Why was he there with Grandma? It was so strange.

I watched as he received a paper being passed around the table. He took a pen and signed his name.

"Who are the rest of the people sitting in the chairs?" I asked.

"We don't know them," Lex replied.

Grandma looked at us both and whispered, "Not yet."

CHAPTER 1

ALEXA

Jay waited eagerly for Tiff and Jen. We stood at the local mall parking lot, which was the designated bus stop for our ride to sleepaway camp. We would soon be on our way to our summer wonderland for the next two months.

Jay gazed at the storefront windows, eyeing her next purchase. I was preoccupied, worried that I'd left my new book at home and had nothing to read on the bus. "Mom, did you put my book in my bag when we packed last night?" I asked.

I looked into Mom's eyes and saw they were filled with tears. Mom nodded, and I knew that she was sad. I assumed it was because this was the first time we were leaving home for more than a few days.

"Lex, let's grab a seat on the bus," Jay hollered.

As we stood in line for the bus, Jay grabbed my arm and looked at me.

"Lex, why are you wearing that dress? It's so passé," she said.

I looked down at my pink floral dress. "I like it," I replied timidly.

Jay looked at me disapprovingly. We're so different. No one ever thinks we're sisters, let alone twins.

I've been told that I take after our Dad and Jay looks like our Mom.

I have long black hair that falls midway down my back and green, almond-shaped eyes, but then there's the big carrot that sticks out in the middle of my face. I always imagined it smaller. Maybe one day....

As I daydreamed, Jay fiddled around with my dress. She took out a hair clip and gathered some of the fabric with it.

"Hey, what did you do that for?" I asked.

"I'm just helping you look more stylish, Lex. You should thank me, at least one of us knows how to be hip," Jay said.

I often felt overshadowed by Jay, because I am more reserved, introverted, and apparently not a fashionista. Although I wanted to be mad at her, in that moment, I couldn't help but notice how forgiving she looked in her red shirtdress.

I gazed at Jay while she texted Tiff as we stood in line. Her blonde curls flowed around her face. Her big, brown, almond-shaped eyes matched the freckles that reappeared from the summer sun and framed her cute button nose. Jay was a cheerleader and the president of our sixth grade class. She sang a rap song instead of making a traditional election speech, and that was the last time she'd worn the red shirtdress.

Jay nudged me and snapped me out of my thoughts. The line moved, and it was our turn to secure our seats. We made our way onto the bus and set our backpacks down. Then we ran back off the bus to see if Tiff and Jen had arrived and to say our good-byes. Jay scampered off ahead and kept a lookout for our two friends.

I had to admit, I was nervous heading off to sleepaway camp for the first time. I really didn't want to go, but Mom and Dad thought it was best so they could spend the summer taking care of Grandma. I didn't know how I was going to do, participating in all the group activities. I was a loner and preferred solo acts, like reading or arts and crafts.

Mom encouraged me to make more friends and try new things, although we had a deal that if I was upset, Mom would resort to our backup plan. In that case, she promised that she would call the camp and request alone time for me.

I crouched down on the cement surface and pulled my backpack off and opened it. I was totally engrossed in my search when I heard his voice by my side.

"What are you looking for, Lex?" he asked.

It was Harold! Actually, he preferred to be called Ghostie Harold. Of course Harold was here. I looked up, and he was holding it: *Lois and Her Very Big Nose*. "My book, Harold, you found it," I said relieved.

Harold waved the book around in the air. "Nice book of choice, Lex," Harold said sarcastically.

I yanked it from his hands and placed it in my backpack, safe and sound. "All right, I guess we're all set to go now," I told him.

Harold had been around us since we were little. He was not my imaginary friend. He was very real to me. Harold's a spirit guide who hangs around Jay and me. Only, Jay can't ever see him, but I usually can.

Ever since Harold came into our lives, he's communicated directly with me. I translated his messages to Jay, when she let me.

Harold told us that he can change sizes and faces whenever he wanted, but he preferred to stay the same height as us. The first time I saw him, I thought he was a "mini" Santa Claus because he had curly gray hair, a big whitish-gray beard, and small eyes with glasses that rested on the end of his nose. He always wore the same outfit: a white button-down shirt, red bowtie, red suspenders, and gray trousers.

I had felt Harold's presence around us my whole life, or for most of what my memory permitted. Harold didn't manifest into human form until I was five years old. It was when our family went on summer vacation to our Mom's hometown of Charleston, South Carolina.

I remember that day clear as can be. I was busy making sand castles on the beach while Jay frolicked around in the ocean with our Dad. I heard a voice call out to me, and it said, "Ouch, stop digging, you're getting my glasses full of sand."

I continued digging, and the voice carried on. It was the same voice that I've heard in my head all along. Then, I dared the voice to let me see him.

Suddenly, he popped out of my castle. As it crumbled apart he spit out a mouthful of sand and said, "Yuck, that tastes awful! Quick, hand me some water to wash it down."

My eyes bulged in disbelief, and all I could do was stumble over my words. "Who are you? How did you get here?" I asked.

"Well, you dared me, didn't you? I never refuse a good dare," he said with a big grin.

I was excited and giggled as he did a dance to shake off the leftover sand.

"Well, it's nice to finally meet you in person, Lex. I am Harold, yours and Jay's spirit guide."

Just like that Harold came into our life, and from that day forth he hasn't strayed too far from our side.

When I introduced Jay to Harold for the first time Harold played peekaboo, thinking he was being endearing. Now, years later, I felt like it was déjà vu. Harold had tried to lighten up my mood by playing peekaboo, only I was too old for that game; plus, it wasn't the right time or place. Harold, not now, I said to myself. I knew he heard me. He reads my thoughts. Harold ignored me and continued his antics.

JAYCEE

"My hair is swaying, my skirt is too tight; my hips are shaking from left to right. Boom shak-a-lak-a boom!" I was cheering in my head because I was so excited that the day was finally here and we were off to sleepaway camp. Two whole months of fun.

What was Lex doing over there? Uh-oh, she's having a conversation on her left side, which meant only one thing, Harold! She was always talking to Harold. Ghostie Harold, Lex often corrected me. I didn't question her senses. I knew Harold was around, but I never saw him. Apparently he talked to Lex constantly.

"Lex," I hollered.

Everyone at the bus stop turned around. Whoops! It worked though, and Lex heard me. I waved my hands frantically in the air, indicating for her to come over.

"What is it, Jay?" Lex said as she took deep breaths.

"Help me look for Tiff and Jen."

Finally, we spotted Tiff in the near distance. Her skin was shimmering a beautiful golden yellow, and I saw it before I even saw her. I knew Tiff and Jen by their beautiful yellow glow. I didn't tell them this, of course, but Lex knew.

I had been seeing skin shimmers ever since I could remember. A skin shimmer is made up of rays of a specific color that outline a person's body. I thought everyone saw them, but apparently not. I wished Lex could see it too.

For some reason I was attracted to people with a yellow skin shimmer. I've always associated this color glow with optimism and positivity.

When I first confided in Mom about seeing skin shimmers we were in the kitchen making breakfast. Well, Mom was cooking breakfast, and I hovered over her and watched as she made my eggs. Then it appeared, first as a silver-white light, and then it formed into a color.

Violet. Mom was violet: intuitive and artistic. It always happened when I least expected it. That day, I told Mom she looked very pretty in violet. She looked down at her dress, bewildered.

"Thank you, sweetheart, but you mean green, my dress is green," Mom corrected.

"No, I mean violet, Mom. You are shimmering violet," I said.

I began doing this often enough that Mom was convinced that I must be color-blind. So, a few days later, she took me to get checked out at the eye doctor.

When my tests came back perfect, I could tell that Mom was perplexed.

Shortly thereafter, when Lex and I were baking chocolate chip cookies in the kitchen, I told Lex that she was radiating pink: sensitive and serene.

Mom whispered to Dad sitting on the couch nearby, "I think our girls have some unexplained gifts."

Dad replied back, "I think it's called big imaginations." They chuckled, amused.

Tiff stood next to us at the camp bus stop. Her brown, bouncy long curls swirled around her doll-like face. When I first met her, I thought she was a spitting image of one of my dolls, which I named Rebecca, with her rosy red cheeks and big blue eyes. When Tiff came for sleepovers, I would always have her hold Rebecca, and I'd laugh about how they could be identical twins.

This day, Tiff's eyes were wide with anticipation, and her shimmer was bigger than normal. Tiff was always so stylish. She adorned her own clothes, which I thought was superfab. I remembered the first time we met in third grade. She wore rhinestones on her clothes, and even her shoes were bedazzled. I loved her shiny wardrobe so much that she began to decorate my clothes too. Today she wore a white ruffle dress with her favorite multicolored rhinestone sandals.

"What's up, Jay?" Tiff asked.

"Tiff! I'm so excited. Why isn't Jen with you?" I asked.

"There she is," Lex said, pointing as Jen's parents' car pulled into a parking spot nearby.

The car door opened wide, and out came Jen. Her short, straight black hair blew around her soft, olive-skinned face. Her brown eyes squinted at us. She's unique – and how could she not be with a mother from China and father from Brazil?

Jen stumbled over a rock. Her clumsiness was endearing. She had obviously forgotten to wear her glasses again. Who would have thought she was one of the best soccer players at our school? She had quick feet; everyone at school called her Twinkle Toes. Sometimes the nickname didn't translate when she was just walking, though.

When I first met Jen, of course she was with Tiff. They came as a pair. They've know each other since they were three, when Tiff's family moved down the street.

"Jay, Lex, is that you over there?" Jen called out.

"Yes, it's us," we said in unison. Jen ran over.

"Oh good, we're all here!" I hollered. "Quick, get your seats on the bus."

Tiff and Jen ran off, and we gave our parents hugs and farewell kisses.

"Let's get this show on the road," I roared.

CHAPTER 2

ALEXA

The bus was finally on its way. The ride was winding and bumpy. Bouncing and turning, the bus went over the mountains and through small towns. I felt my ears stuff up from the high altitude.

I took my nose out of my book, looked over Jay's shoulder, and saw the view that she kept oohing and aahing over.

We were on a curvy mountain road above the ocean. I watched the water glisten as the sun's rays hit it perfectly.

We drove deep into the thick of tall redwood trees. Then I saw it: a white picket fence like the one Mom showed us in the brochure, and a giant red sign that welcomed us to Camp In-Between.

I waited until the very last person was gone before I made my way off the bus.

"Lex, Lex," Jay called out to me.

She stood with a husky woman, with curly red hair, whose shirt said camp headmaster.

The headmaster greeted me with her clipboard in hand. "Hello, dear, welcome to Camp In-Between. I'm Mrs. Miller. What's your name, sweetie?"

"Alexa Barron, but I prefer to be called Lex," I said. I looked around for Jay. Suddenly, she was nowhere in sight.

"Nice to meet you, Lex. Let's see here, ..." Mrs. Miller combed through her clipboard. "Alexa Barron, you are in the Arcturus bunk. Your counselor is Celeste."

A beautiful brunette teenager appeared. I guessed she was about eighteen or nineteen, something like that. She was lanky and had shiny, chestnut-colored straight hair, freckles like Jay, hazel almond-shaped eyes, and a nice smile. She was so pretty and feminine. I wanted to look like her when I grew up. I was drawn to her instantly.

Celeste put her arms around me and said, "Hello there Lex, I'm Celeste. I hear you have a twin sister, Jaycee, right? Where is she?"

"Hi Celeste. Yes, Jay is here somewhere," I said and looked around. "There she is," I pointed. "That's Jay."

Jay, Tiff, and Jen were giggling and gawking at some of the boys coming off the buses. Boy crazy, I thought.

"Well, let's go grab them and get you girls settled in," Celeste said.

"Jay, over here," I called out. "We're all in the same bunk." The girls gathered around Celeste and me.

"Arcturus, what a funny name," Tiff said to Celeste and giggled loudly.

"Yes, it's totally weird," Jen chimed in.

Celeste gave a knowing smile and assembled our group together – fourteen girls in all – and led us up the rolling hills to our home for the next two months. We stopped in front of an orange bunk.

"Here we are. Welcome, to bunk Arcturus, girls," Celeste announced.

"Orange?" Jay questioned.

"Yes, it's the color of our star. I'll explain," Celeste announced.

We all convened in front of the bunk. I took a seat on the grass and stared at our orange summer home.

"The bunks at Camp In-Between are named after stars and constellations. Tonight, once we all get settled, we'll be heading to the camp's very own planetarium where we'll see Arcturus and other stars and nebulas you will come to know. Sirius, Vega, Canopus, and Orion are some," Celeste said.

"Oh wow!" Jen said. "My brother has a telescope at home. He would think this is supercool."

"Jen's brother is also supercute," Jay laughed.

"Hey, off limits!" Jen said.

The girls giggled at the thought of boys. All I could think about was the planetarium. I thought about the stars all the time.

"Okay girls, calm down. The whole camp will be joining us tonight. There is a special event planned, and it will be a nice chance for you all to get to know each other and take the time to experience what Camp In-Between is all about. Now let's head into the bunk and get unpacked. I have pizzas waiting inside," Celeste said.

CHAPTER 3

JAYCEE

The sky was a wicked purple hue, and the grass was orange and red. The cows grazed. They had green spots instead of black ones, and a giant dragon flew overhead. I painted the picture in my mind and drew a sun around it daydreaming, as we waited in line to enter the planetarium.

"Jaycee, Earth to Jaycee?" Tiff stood in front of me and snapped her fingers in my face with our new friend and bunkmate, Vee-Vee.

Vee-Vee was African American and had an amazing green skin shimmer. Green, as I know it to be, represents a balanced and nurturing person. As soon as I saw her I wanted to be her friend. Lex liked her too.

Vee-Vee's hair was full and curly, her voice a little raspy like mine, and she accessorized with a lot of yellow: yellow socks, yellow headbands, and yellow jewelry.

"Jay, our bunk is being called to go inside. We want to make sure we all sit together," Vee-Vee said. "I'll go find Lex to make sure she's with us."

I liked that Vee-Vee looked out for Lex and wanted to be her friend. I smiled to myself while Tiff latched onto my arm.

"Look at the large silver dome," Tiff said, and grinned with excitement.

The camp's planetarium sat on top of the highest hill in the camp. It had a huge dome that jutted out over the ground, and the ocean sparkled just below. The line started to move as we headed inside. I looked around and spotted Vee-Vee, who led Lex and Jen over to us.

"Girls, come on we're going in," I called out.

I looked at Lex smiling. I winked at her and smiled back. I knew she would be excited about this. Lex loved the stars. She tapped her cheek three times. That was our signal for Harold. Uh-oh, I thought. Harold was there, and I knew that Lex wanted to tell me what he said.

I made a hand signal back to her, placing my hand to my neck, which indicated for her to cut it out. Her smile faded, and she frowned. I didn't want to make Lex feel bad, but I wasn't going to talk about Harold just then.

We shuffled into the planetarium. The ceiling was a retractable roof and it was open, letting in the night sky. Celeste led us over to an open area dedicated to our bunk. We took our seats on the soft squishy floor.

Lex sat down next to me and tugged my arm. "Hey, I didn't want to tell you about Harold but he's trying to get our attention. He wants you to go to the telescope. He won't stop talking about it, Jay. Just go over there, he's being very persistent," Lex said.

"Shh, Lex, not now," I whispered. Why did she have to talk about him with all these people around?

"Jay, I'm not kidding. Please go over to the telescope or he's not going to leave me alone."

I knew that if I didn't go to the telescope, *Lex* wasn't going to leave *me* alone. I gave her a frustrated look and rolled my eyes. "I can't believe you are doing this now," I said.

Lex pointed toward the telescopes off to the side. "They're just a few feet away," Lex persisted.

Some campers were already using them. "Okay Lex, if I go, you and Harold are coming with me," I said.

Together, we walked over to them. I turned to Lex. She gave me a big smile because I was willing to participate in her communications with Harold. Lex looked over to her left side, where she claimed Harold was usually located.

One of the campers finished, and the purple telescope became free. Finally, it was my turn. I leaned in and put my eye on the metal surface and focused the scope. I saw an amazing array of stars, bright and colorful.

"They're so close I want to reach out and touch them, Lex. This is amazing," I said.

"Harold says to look carefully and relax your eyes," Lex directed.

"Okay, I am," I replied, following Harold's lead. "What am I supposed to see?" I asked.

"Just look again and tell us what appears," Lex instructed.

I took a second glance, and then the stars started to do a little dance. It was similar to what I see before a skin shimmer appears. It usually starts off as a soft glow, and then gets bigger and brighter, eventually forming a color. This was different, though. The stars were moving around, and it looked like they were trying to connect to each other.

"Wait, what's going on here? The stars are wiggling and repositioning," I said, confused.

"Harold says to continue, keep telling us what happens," Lex advised.

"The stars are rearranging themselves in the sky. I think they are trying to communicate something? I see letters in the stars, but I can't make out any words...," I said.

"Look again! Harold says there is a message for us," Lex insisted.

A woman's voice came over the loudspeakers. "Testing, testing 1-2-3," she said.

"Lex, Jay, come join the bunk," Celeste called out to both of us.

"Oh no, we have to go," Lex frowned.

As the dome slowly closed, the woman's voice came over the loudspeakers again. "Okay campers, settle down and find your seats. I hope everyone is really excited for our first night at Camp In-Between."

"Uh-oh. Lex, we'll have to do this later. It's starting," I said.

Lex was not happy about it. I was too excited about the show to be distracted by Harold's communications.

Everyone cheered loudly as Mrs. Miller stepped up on her podium of milk crates and addressed the camp. "Good evening, Camp In-Between! What a terrific summer this is going to be. First, I'd like to welcome our new campers."

Whistles and applause filled the air. I smiled at Lex and hugged her warmly, my way of apologizing for dismissing Harold earlier.

Mrs. Miller continued, "Also, I'd like to thank our veteran campers for coming back to be a part of our family. As you see new faces, make sure to say hello. Now let's start off this summer right and all chant our camp cheer!" Mrs. Miller started clapping her hands rapidly.

Everyone stood up shouting and whistling. "On the count of three," Mrs. Miller directed, "1-2-3."

HEY, HEY, THE GANG'S ALL HERE!
WELCOME TO CAMP IN-BE-TWEEN.
NESTLED NEXT TO THE MOUNTAINS AND THE SEA.
THE MOUNTAINS AND THE SEA,
IT'S WHERE YOU WANT TO BE.
FROM STAR TO STAR, THIS IS WHO WE ARE.
THE GANG'S ALL HERE,
WELCOME TO CAMP IN-BETWEEN!

We repeated the cheer again. Tiff was jumping up and down. I spun Lex around, and Jen and Vee-Vee bumped their hips together and clapped their hands.

Mrs. Miller calmed the room back down and announced, "Let the light show begin."

The room went dark, and then the inside of the dome lit up above us with an image mimicking the night sky. Everyone quieted down as we watched it begin to glow with stars, constellations, and distant galaxies in beautiful colors of hot pink, green, blue, and gold.

I looked over to Lex, who was mesmerized. She smiled at me. I turned back, but I was sidetracked, because I spotted something out of the corner of my eye. It was a turquoise blue shimmer. I was surprised to see that shade of blue. I associated that with a person who is compassionate and creative.

I followed the shimmer to a boy with curly blond hair, who was staring at me from across the way. We caught each other's gaze, and he quickly turned away.

He was so cute. I thought he was in the Canopus bunk, but he was too far away, so I couldn't read the sign. I squinted, but that didn't help much. The night-sky projections continued, and Mrs. Miller was in the process of showing the camp some of the stars and constellations in the sky connected to the names of each bunk.

"Arcturus," Mrs. Miller called out, and zoomed in on a big, bright orange-colored star.

"Woo-hoo, that's us!" I shouted.

Vee-Vee, Tiff, and Jen hollered loudly. We stood and put our hands high up in the air, and I could see the name of the sign. Yup, just what I thought. He was in the Canopus bunk.

"Canopus!" Mrs. Miller called out.

The boys applauded loudly, and the blond-haired boy looked at me again. I cheered. The light show continued as Mrs. Miller gave shout-outs to the other bunks.

I grabbed Lex's hand and whispered, "Is Harold watching this?"

Lex looked at me surprised and nodded. I think we both wondered about the message Harold wanted us to see.

The sky lit up again. I saw the campers' shimmers form an array of colors all around us. The room was illuminated inside and out. I soaked it all in and beamed.

CHAPTER 4

ALEXA

Music blasted through the speakers on the walls. The reveille call had officially begun. I looked at the clock – ugh, it was only seven in the morning. I pulled my pillow over my head. I was not ready to get up.

"C'mon girls, get up, get up, big day ahead. It's time to go to breakfast and then instructional swim. Put on your bathing suits now 'cause there will be no time to change in between," Celeste said.

Jay plopped onto my bed. It shook back and forth. "Wake up sleepy head, it's the first day of camp," she said cheerfully.

"Okay Jay, I'm up, stop shaking the bed," I said.

I made my way over to my shelf and got dressed. We lined up at the front door. Celeste took a head count. I waited for Jay, but she never came to my side. She found Tiff and Jen and walked with them. I followed at the back of the line.

It was white tee day for the Arcturus bunk. Every bunk was assigned a color, and that's the camp tee that we wore for the day. For each color there was a matching girl and boy bunk, and we got to socialize with them during certain activities. That was how Camp In-Between worked.

I overheard Celeste say to Marcie, counselor of the Vega bunk, that the Canopus boys were joining us at swim.

As we walked to breakfast, I couldn't help but notice the breathtaking scenery. Over to the left was the ocean, and to the right there were rows and rows of green mountains. Our camp was nestled in-between; hence, its name, I presumed.

We walked down the rolling green hills and past the crystal blue lake filled with paddleboats and kayaks. We turned left onto a winding cement path and approached the blue cabin known as the mess hall.

The inside of it reminded me of a log cabin rather than a cafeteria, because the walls and ceiling were covered in wood. There was a large buffet over to the side, and long tables with benches filled the remaining space.

Celeste brought us to our table, designated with a small sign in red letters that said Arcturus.

"Here we are girls, this is our spot. Go ahead, get in line and grab your food, and we'll meet back here," Celeste said.

Jay waited for me to accompany her. She always liked to see what I was going to eat. I filled my plate up with pancakes and fresh fruit. Jay took scrambled eggs and potatoes.

We sat down at the table. Celeste was in mid-conversation with Vee-Vee, and I overheard her say, "Everyone will have to take a swim test once we get to the pool."

Swim test, oh no, tests made me nervous. I had to think of some way to get out of it quickly. I thought about it while I ate my pancakes.

"Arcturus girls, line up, it's time to head to the pool," Celeste instructed.

We left the mess hall and walked down the hill toward the large swimming pool. The lifeguard was already situated on his tall chair. I opened my oversized towel on the green grass. Jay spread out hers next to mine, took off her bracelets, and placed them on her towel. Then she ran over to a group of girls huddled together. They were staring and pointing at the Canopus boys making their way over to the pool.

I was not interested. I felt too awkward to be into boys. Maybe once my face grew to catch up with my nose – at least that's what Mom always assured me would happen.

I let out a hopeful sigh, as I lingered on that thought for a moment or two. I felt the cool breeze and goose bumps appeared on my arms, which brought me back to the reality of where I was.

The morning dew was still on the grass, and the air from the mountains was crisp. I was chilly. None of the other girls seemed to mind. They stripped down to their bathing suits.

Jay came over strutting around in her new yellow two-piece. She stopped right in front of me and posed with her hands on her hips. "What do you think, Lex?"

Jay was blocking out the sun. My teeth chattered, and I said, "It matches your curls." I gave her a half smile.

I looked at Jay, and her eyes were fixed on the Canopus boys nearby. Her eyes grew wider and wider, and she ran off with Tiff and Jen.

"Celeste," I called out, waving my hands frantically.

"What is it, Lex? Is everything okay?" she asked.

Before I called Celeste over, I made sure to sit in a spot directly in the sun and let the rays hit my face, making it flush and warm. This was something Jay taught me a long time ago when she didn't want to go to school.

"Not really," I said. "I don't feel too well." I held my stomach and placed my hands over my head.

Celeste pushed my hand away and placed hers against my forehead. "Hmm, you do seem a bit warm to me. Just to be safe, let's go ahead and take you to the infirmary. I'm concerned."

Celeste helped me up and we walked from the pool over to a small little cabin marked with a red cross.

"I'll be back in just a minute," Celeste pointed to the infirmary as she called out to Craig, Canopus' lead counselor.

Craig gave us a big smile and said, "Sure no problem, go ahead. Everything here is under control," as one of his boys threw another one into the pool.

The whistle blew. "Hey, no pushing!" Scott the lifeguard hollered.

A petite blond nurse wearing a white cap greeted us at the door of the infirmary. Celeste left me there and headed back to the pool.

CHAPTER 5

JAYCEE

"Cannonball!" I screamed as I jumped into the shallow end of the pool. This was so not allowed, and I knew it. I made the biggest splash ever and laughed as I landed right next to Jen, and her glasses went flying off.

"Jay, stop that!" she shrieked and grabbed her glasses quickly before they sank to the bottom.

"Sorry, Jen." A whistle blew, and I thought I might be in trouble.

"Jaycee," I heard a man's voice, confirming that I was. "Out of the pool," Scott, the really cute lifeguard said.

I hadn't meant to cause any trouble.

"Jaycee." Scott was standing in front of me. "You are not allowed to jump from the shallow end. You've lost pool privileges for the day."

"I'm sorry," I said. I saw everyone staring at me, and I blushed a little. I guessed I shouldn't have done that. Scott handed me my towel, and I found a place on the grass.

Tiff splashed around in the water with Jen, and they made funny faces at me. I sat down on the grass and soaked up the sun. Scott arranged everyone into groups for the swim test.

"That's a nice cannonball you've got there," I heard a voice say.

I opened my eyes and saw him standing above me. Oh wow, it was the blond boy from the planetarium, I screamed in my head. Stay calm, stay calm. I was hoping he'd talk to me.

He had the gentlest baby blue eyes I had ever seen. He was at least a foot taller than I and his wavy blond hair blew in his face a little as he smiled, waiting for me to respond. But I couldn't because close up his skin shimmer was more beautiful than I had noticed before. It was radiant and the only other turquoise shimmer I've ever seen aside from my own. I smiled so big my mouth hurt.

"Thanks, my brother and I do them all the time at home in our pool. I'm Jaycee, but Jay for short."

He returned my big smile. "I'm Danny. You want some company, or will I get in trouble too?" He laughed.

"I don't know. Sit at your own risk. If Scott comes over here, just stop talking and look the other way, then he won't see you," I said in my most flirtatious voice.

Danny squinted in confusion. "Do you think that will work?"

He was so cute I couldn't keep a straight face. I laughed. "Well, I think sometimes if you don't see people, they won't see you. I call it my invisible force field of the antiseeing tactic."

"What? Say again?" Danny was intrigued.

"It's simple, but complicated."

"Okay well, if you say so, I'll try it," he smiled.

As we talked, I learned that Danny was two years older than I, and he was going into the eighth grade. He preferred sweet potato fries over regular fries (like me), and he liked to paint and play soccer. Paint? Did he just say paint?

"I love to paint," I giggled.

"Well, maybe we can ask our bunks to be paired up for a paint party," he smiled.

Just when our conversation couldn't get any better, Tiff and Jen ran over dripping wet from the pool.

"Guess who is in the dolphin swim group?" Jen said proudly.

Before I could respond, Tiff interjected.

"Jay, looks like you're not in trouble any more, huh?" Tiff said, squeezing water from her hair on me.

I jumped up. "Hey, what's that for? It's cold!" I was startled.

Tiff laughed with Jen. She looked at Danny. It felt awkward. Why was Tiff being weird? Her skin shimmer had turned a bit darker, a muddy yellow, like mustard, which wasn't a good sign.

"Hi, you're Danny right?" Tiff asked.

I watched Tiff as she introduced herself to my soon-to-be boyfriend. Maybe she just felt left out.

I interrupted them with a blast of excitement. "Hey Tiff, guess what? Danny says we can ask for our bunks to team up for a painting party. How cool would that be?"

Tiff's mood lightened up a bit, and both girls sat down. Danny called a few of his friends over to join us, but I noticed Tiff's eyes were fixed on Danny. That upset me. After all, he had come over to sit next to me. The whistle blew, indicating swim was over.

"Okay, little ladies, wrap it up," Celeste announced.

Craig was collecting the campers out of the pool, and we said our good-byes.

"So, paint party then?" Danny questioned.

"Totally!" Tiff and I said simultaneously.

"Sure!" Jen confirmed.

"Cool, I'll ask my counselor, Craig, to hook it up with Celeste," Danny said excitedly.

Danny looked at me. "I'll make sure to try the antiseeing tactic later and let you know how it goes," he winked.

I blushed. "Shh, don't say it too loud." I giggled.

He smiled and ran off to join his bunk.

"What's he talking about?" Jen asked.

I grinned and shrugged.

"Well, I think he is supercute! Did you see his dimples?" Tiff said.

"Yeah..." I trailed off, not knowing how to respond.

"Ladies!" Celeste called out from the gate.

I looked around and suddenly realized that Lex was nowhere in sight. Had she been gone for all of swim time?

"Where's Lex?" I asked.

ALEXA

Nurse Anne walked toward my cot. She hunched over and rubbed my arm. "How are you feeling, sweetie?"

"Better," I said.

"Swim time is over," Nurse Anne confirmed.

"May I call my Mom, please?" I asked politely.

"Sure, I guess, but only on this one occasion because you're not feeling well, otherwise you have to wait for the time that you are assigned by your counselor, Celeste."

Nurse Anne handed me the phone and walked away to check on another camper.

"Hello?" Mom answered.

"Mom," I whispered, hoping she could still hear me.

"Well, hi there Lex, how's camp? I wasn't expecting it to be you," she said.

"Mom, I'm at the nurse, please listen while I talk quickly."

"The nurse? Are you okay, Lex?"

"Yes, but the camp is making us swim and do all these things that I don't like to do. Please Mom can you call up and let me have some alone time, to read my book and maybe arts and crafts?"

"But Lex, it's good for you to try new things and spend time with other girls your age," she said.

"I am, I will, I promise, I just really don't want to have to swim in a cold pool at 9:00am."

"9:00am," Mom repeated. "Hmm, okay, I will call the camp for you and see what can be arranged," she assured me.

"Thanks Mom, you're the best. Can you call now, please?"

"Alright, hon, I will do it now, before I forget."

I hung up the phone. I couldn't hide my big smug grin. Celeste was back at the door. "How are we doing Lex, any better?"

I nodded my head. Celeste grabbed my hand. I could feel her warm energy.

We walked back to the pool, well, just outside the gate.

"Lex, Lex you're back!" Jen said, jumping up and down.

Mrs. Miller approached Celeste.

"Celeste," she called out from a few feet away. "Can I speak to you for a moment?"

"Sure," Celeste answered.

Celeste and Mrs. Miller walked a few steps away, out of earshot.

I watched silently. Jen, Tiff, and Jay were all gushing about the cute boys in the Canopus bunk. I heard names being mentioned: Danny, Tommy, Alex. Tiff said, "Maybe Abe for Lex?"

My eyes were focused on Celeste and Mrs. Miller. I had a hunch I knew what this was all about. Thanks, Mom, I thought, letting out a big sigh of relief.

Tiff glanced at me and assumed it was a sigh of love. "Oh good, so Lex you like Abe?" Tiff questioned.

I didn't want the girls to know that I called home, so I just said, "Yeah, sure I guess."

Mrs. Miller walked away and Celeste came back. "Arcturus bunk, let's get on our way. It's time for our next activity," Celeste announced proudly.

Celeste called me to the front of the line and grabbed my hand again. We all walked together on the cement path that wrapped around the boat lake.

"Celeste!" Jay hollered. "I met one of the boys from the Canopus bunk, Danny, and we talked about having a painting party together. Please can we? He said that you have to talk to his counselor, Craig. Could you please talk to Craig, Celeste?" Jay begged.

Celeste smiled a little. "Okay, Jay, I'll look into that for you girls. We've done those before."

"You're the best," Jay declared and ran off to share the news with the girls.

Celeste squeezed my hand to get my attention discretely and whispered, "Mrs. Miller informed me that your Mom called the camp. They are going to give you more alone time, electives. That's what you want right, Lex?"

I stuttered and said quietly, "Well, yes, I guess."

Celeste squeezed my hand again, a gesture to let me know she understood. "You know when I was your age, I felt the same way. I liked to be alone, and sometimes I would just sit, relax, and listen to music. You know it's okay to have time by yourself."

Wow. I was surprised that Celeste was just like me. Sometimes, I felt like an outcast because I liked to be by myself. Mom and Jay were always pushing me to socialize with other girls. Sometimes, I just didn't want to, so I was glad Mom empathized with me this time.

I squeezed Celeste's hand a little tighter and noticed her wrist was adorned with beautiful orange glass beads. I counted four strands. "I love your bracelets. I've never seen beads like that before," I said.

Celeste smiled. "They might look like several bracelets, but they're actually one long strand."

"Really?" I questioned.

Celeste unwrapped the strand from her wrist and held the beads in her hand. I stared at them. They were all different shades of orange, mostly coral.

"I use these beads to help me relax. I call them worry beads. When I feel anxious or scared, I unravel my worry beads and roll them in my hands," Celeste said.

"Worry beads. I like them. I wonder if my Mom can send me some." I said.

"Maybe you should hold onto these for me." Celeste insisted. She took the beads and rolled them around my wrist.

"Really? Are you sure?" I asked.

"Yes, I'd like you to keep them safe for me. I will show you how to use them when I take you to Think Time."

"Think Time?" I questioned.

Celeste smiled and squeezed my hand again. "It's the alone time you wanted. I'll take you there tomorrow."

I gave her a hug. I felt better already.

CHAPTER 6

ALEXA

I stared at the worry beads adorning my wrist. I couldn't wait to learn more about them at Think Time. Celeste led us over a small, wooden pedestrian bridge. Below us was a koi pond.

"The koi pond is also known as the wishing well. For over twenty years campers have come with a coin in hand," Celeste said.

"What do you do with the coin?" Vee-Vee asked.

"Well, the legend at Camp In-Between is that you are supposed to close your eyes and make a wish. You set your intentions and say a special rhyme for the universe to hear before you release the coin and see if it grants you your wish. And it goes like this..."

A thought, a hope, a wish, a dream.
I ask for help, my fish agleam:
This coin holds my intentions.
Take them through vast dimensions.
Return them here—Camp In-Between.

"I like that," said Vee-Vee.

"According to the legend, not all wishes come true. It all depends on how the coin lands. If it lands in the right spot, your wish will be granted," Celeste advised.

"Can we make some wishes at the well?" asked Jen.

"Not right now, girls, but don't worry we will," Celeste assured us. "It's time for lunch."

CHAPTER 7

JAYCEE

"A little birdie in a tree!"[i]
I hollered as we walked through a large field toward the mess hall. I started a cheer; I loved doing that. I ran up to the front of the group. Everyone should know this one. I grabbed Tiff's hand to lead it with me. Everyone chimed in, and we all sang.

A little birdie in a tree.
Says something very true to me.
Says something very true to me.
He says Arcturus is the best.
Better than all the rest.
Sound off.
1, 2.
Sound off.
3, 4.
Bring it on down.
1, 2, 3, 4.[ii]

All the girls clapped, cheered, and whistled as we arrived at the mess hall. "Whoo, what a rush, I am starved," I laughed.

"Come on ladies, let's find our spot," Celeste said.

Celeste took a head count to make sure we were all there.

Lex skipped over to me, and we went to the buffet line. We filled our plates with grilled chicken and veggies.

The food in the mess hall was organic and prepared more like at a restaurant than a camp cafeteria. I didn't like a lot of greasy food. I didn't eat bread because I had a gluten sensitivity.

Mom was worried about what I'd be able to eat, so she promised she would send me packages every week filled with my favorite treats. When we arrived at camp, Lex and I already had three boxes waiting at our bunk.

Wait, what's that, I wondered. Tunnel vision was all I had as I saw a familiar shimmer just up ahead. It was him!

Danny looked so cute in his white Camp In-Between T-shirt and green cargo shorts. He was just a few feet away, and he hadn't seen me yet.

I quickly whispered in Lex's ear, "Don't look now, but there's a boy with curly blond hair and green shorts on the burger line. That's Danny."

Lex looked over anyway.

"I told you not to look!" I said, and tugged her arm.

"Ouch, Jay, relax, I didn't even get to see him. I'll look later. Who's Danny anyway?"

My shoulders rolled up and I had a big grin. "I really like him ... and he's turquoise," I said.

Lex understood this and smiled. "Harold likes him too," Lex confirmed.

I ignored that as I watched Tiff cut in front of Danny to get a burger. Tiff didn't even like burgers. She was flirting. I could tell by the way she tossed her hair around. She fumbled with her tray; Danny grabbed it and helped her off the line. I gasped.

Lex saw that and said, "Looks like Tiff fancies him too."

Neither Danny nor Tiff saw us, or at least I didn't think so. Lex and I took a seat at the table.

The Canopus boys pounded the table with their fists, signaling for everyone's attention.

They chanted:

Announcements, Announcements![iii]

All the campers in the mess hall chanted back excitedly:

Announcements, Announcements!

Craig, the Canopus counselor, stood up and whistled loudly. "Campers, listen up! Bunk Canopus is going to host a special event." Everyone cheered. My eyes bulged. I hoped it was what I thought it was.

Craig continued, "Join us for a campwide social. It will be a dance and painting party in the rec hall. So, if you want to paint, make sure to tell your counselor to sign you up."

Cheers and applause filled the room. Craig sat back down, and everyone in the mess hall resumed conversation.

Marcie, the Vega bunk counselor, leaned over to Celeste and said, "We want to chant back to the boys' announcement with the 'Awesome'[iv] song on three. Celeste, can you get your bunk to join in with us?"

"Surely," Celeste responded to Marcie.

"Arcturus girls, 'Awesome' on three. Follow my lead, 1-2-3." Celeste said. Celeste began the cheer:

A-W-E-S-O-M-E
Awesome, awesome, awesome
Is bunk Canopus![v]

We all repeated the chant one more time together. He'd gotten us a paint party! I was so excited. It was exactly what Danny and I were talking about at the pool.

I looked around the table and saw Tiff and Jen staring at me smiling. Maybe Tiff was just being nice to him? I didn't know, but I was too thrilled to care. I ran through my wardrobe in my head and thought about what I should wear to catch Danny's attention.

I glanced over at the Canopus table and locked eyes with Danny. I blushed. He gave me a thumbs-up, and I drew a heart around his face in my mind. I couldn't wait. I'd have a whole night to hang out with Danny. I returned the thumbs-up. I smiled to myself and continued to drift off, surrendering to my thoughts. I was so happy that Mom and Dad sent us to camp.

CHAPTER 8

ALEXA

Click, clack. Click, clack, the sound of girls' shoes meeting the bunk's wooden floor. I was lying on my bed. I held the worry beads in my hands and rolled them through my fingers as I read my book. I felt anxious because I missed home.

I continued to rub my beads. I wasn't sure if they were working yet, but I kept trying.

Thump. Jay belly-flopped on my bed.

"Hey, what did you do that for?!" I said.

"Whatcha got there Lex?" Jay asked.

Before I could answer, Jay took my book and looked at the title.

"*Lois and Her Very Big Nose.*" Jay rolled her eyes, tossed the book on the floor, and yanked me out of the bed. "Let's go, you're getting into the shower, and we are dressing you up for the dance party tonight. There will be lots of cute boys."

I was out of bed, thanks to Jay. I took my glasses off, grabbed my robe and basket of toiletries, and headed over to the showers.

Click clack, click clack, tap, tap. I heard the sounds of the Arcturus girls hanging over the bathroom vanities, moving around in their shoes and doing their hair. There was an army of hair dryers, flat irons, and curlers plugged into the wall.

I walked out of the shower in my robe. My hair was dripping wet. I put it up with a towel.

Jay turned toward me while curling her hair.

"Lex, how do I look? Do you think I should change my outfit?" Jay asked.

"No, I think you look great," I said.

She did, she always did. Jay was wearing one of her supertrendy royal blue ruffled miniskirts with a white tank top, accessorized with a tan roped belt and matching wedge sandals.

I apathetically walked toward my designated shelf. Jay came over and yanked on my hair. "Ouch! That hurts!" I shrieked.

Jay blew her dryer on my hair, and I didn't resist: I knew whatever she did would come out well. She was much better than me at all that stuff. Jay pinned the last curler in my hair, while all the girls scurried to pack up their stuff.

"Girls, its time, hurry up and let's go," Celeste declared.

"Lex, your hair looks great. You think you can handle the rest?" Jay asked.

"Sure, yeah I like it. Thanks Jay," I said.

Celeste saw me standing in my robe and said, "Sweetie, you want us to wait for you?"

"No, I can meet you all there. I hope that's okay?" I asked.

"Well, I don't really feel comfortable leaving you alone in the bunk. Marcie is next door still getting ready, so I will tell her to check on you. If I don't see you at the rec hall in fifteen minutes, I am going to come here and get you, okay?" Celeste assured me.

"Okay, deal," I responded.

The door slammed shut. I walked toward my bed and saw my outfit all laid out. Jay handpicked it before she left. It was totally not me at all, but I was already late and didn't have time to find something else. I trusted Jay's style, so I decided to try it out.

CHAPTER 9

JAYCEE

My heart was racing. I couldn't get to the rec hall fast enough. I wanted to look my most adorable, even though I knew we would be painting. This time I didn't care if I got my outfit dirty, because it was a chance to get to know Danny.

I was so excited that I tried to run down the hill, but the best I could do was shuffle in my wedges. I held hands with Tiff, Jen, and Vee-Vee. A cute little foursome we were. I hoped Lex got there soon.

Celeste led us toward the door, and all I could think about was Danny. Where was he? Would he like how I looked? Did he really want to paint with me? I glanced over at Tiff and wondered if she was thinking the same thing.

"Jay! I'm really psyched to paint, but do you think we'll get dirty? I just made this dress and I don't want to ruin it," Tiff asked.

Tiff looked great in her asymmetric red dress, adorned with black rhinestones and black and white polka dot wedges. Her hair was pinned back, and curls drooped down her back.

"I hope not. You look so cute Tiff. I love that dress," I smiled.

Jen and Vee-Vee decided to wear matching black miniskirts and cropped black tanks. They also had matching yellow accessories. Compliments of Vee-Vee, I assumed. They had a plan to spice up their outfits with paint.

Craig greeted us at the door and handed us our painting aprons.

"Well, I guess you'll be safe with these, Tiff," I laughed.

Tiff happily took her apron. Jen and Vee-Vee both declined that option.

"Okay girls, suit yourselves," Craig said to Vee-Vee and Jen. He looked at me. "Hey, Jay, I know someone wanted you to have these."

Craig handed me a special paintbrush and tube full of paint. I looked down at the label. Turquoise.

Turquoise? But how did he know? Craig smiled, waiting for me to ask who, but of course I already knew.

"Oh, um thanks, I can't wait. How does this all work anyway?" I asked Craig.

"Well, come on in and I'll show you," Craig said, and led me inside.

The music was playing, and strobe lights flashed around the room. Easels were set up along the perimeter of the large dance floor that took up the majority of the space. Campers were already lined up waiting to paint on the canvases. A DJ was stationed on a platform in the far back corner, and a table full of delicious treats and refreshments awaited its takers. I saw the cupcakes and knew that Lex would appreciate those.

Craig led me over to a clipboard where campers were busy searching for their names.

"Everyone can sign up for a time to paint at this board, and at the end of the night we'll raffle off the canvases," Craig said, smiling.

"Oh, that's so great. Yes, I told Celeste I wanted to paint, but I don't think I am registered yet," I said.

Craig smiled again. "Well little lady, I think somebody has already taken care of that for you." Craig's finger ran down the list of names. "Here you are. You and Danny are all set to paint together in an hour from now," Craig said, looking at his watch.

My heart fluttered, and I was speechless – which rarely ever happened to me. I thought that it was the best moment of my whole life, and just then I heard a familiar voice.

"Hey, you," Danny said.

I turned to look into the eyes of my sweet crush. There was something about those big blue eyes, something familiar and warm. I wanted to lay down in a field full of sunflowers with those eyes, watching seagulls dip in and out of our very own chocolate-flavored ocean.

"Jay?" Danny asked, trying to get my attention.

I must have drifted off again. Back to reality. "Danny, Danny, I'm so excited! How did you know?" I asked.

"What do you mean, know what? You said you liked to paint right?" He was smiling so big.

"Yes, but the paint?" I held up the turquoise bottle and showed it to him.

"Turquoise?" I asked, with a smile bigger than his.

My mouth hurt again. He gazed at me in a different way. He looked past me. I peeked over my left shoulder but no one was there. I realized the only other thing it could be.

"Hey, you guys," my trio called from a few feet away. Before I knew it, Tiff had her arm wrapped around Danny. What was she doing?

"Let's dance!" Jen screamed.

Tiff caught my eye and grabbed my hand. "Come on Jay, you promised me one. Let's go do our favorite dance," Tiff said.

Danny shrugged, indicating he thought it was a good idea.

"Come on, Danny," Tiff said, and she took his hand and dropped mine.

Tiff ran off to the dance floor with Danny. I brushed my shoulders off. Two could play at this game.

CHAPTER 10

ALEXA

I caught a glimpse of myself in the mirror before I headed over to the rec hall. Jay had worked wonders with her curling iron. She'd placed my hair in big bouncy curls that lightly rested on my shoulders. I wore a red miniskirt and a white tank top. That outfit was a vast departure from my usual look. It was one of Jay's creations that she fanatically assured me would look great.

I walked out the door and headed down the hill. I saw the lights from the rec hall in the near distance.

Something was tickling my wrist. I glanced down, and it was a beautiful blue and purple butterfly, perched on me. This was strange. Why was a butterfly out at night and sitting on me? I never saw one up close like that. Its pattern was magnificent. I walked carefully, so as not to disturb her, and she accompanied me to the rec hall.

Just as I arrived at the front door, she fluttered around me and then flew away. I smiled to myself. I'd enjoyed her company.

I opened the doors. The music was loud, and campers were running all around. It was very festive and inviting. The beautiful lights were enough to keep me there, and everyone was laughing and dancing.

"Hey Lex, you made it. Where have you been?" Vee-Vee asked.

"Oh hey, I had a slow start getting ready," I said quietly.

"Cool, well you look superpretty. I've never seen you all dressed up," Vee-Vee said, smiling.

I really liked Vee-Vee. Two boys looked over at us and waved hello.

"Do you know them?" I asked Vee-Vee.

"No, but I think they like your skirt," she said, spinning me around.

I was a little embarrassed. I pulled my skirt down a bit. "I don't know about this. Jay made me wear it," I said.

"Oh stop it. Own it, girl! Come on, let's check out what's going on over there." Vee-Vee pulled my arm to follow her.

A small circle had formed on the dance floor. It was too hard to tell what was going on. I looked around for Jay, but I didn't see her.

Campers cheered and clapped as they watched someone dancing in the center. It was Jay. Of course it was.

She was magnetic and drew in the whole room with her swanky dance moves. The ruffles from her skirt swung in the air. Jay was doing a type of dance she called "street dancing." It looked like break dancing, but Jay said it's not since she couldn't spin on her head. My eyes were fixed on her, and I noticed that Danny was watching her too. One of his friends nudged him, and he smiled. I looked over and saw Tiff staring from across the room. Uh-oh, something was wrong. Tiff whispered something to Jen. Hmm, I wondered why Tiff wasn't dancing with Jay like they always did?

The song was over, and the circle thinned out. Danny approached Jay, grabbed her hand and spun her around. I found a nice little spot in the corner and watched their interaction.

Jay twirled her blonde curls around her fingers and gazed into Danny's blue eyes. I saw Tiff staring at them. Her eyes bore a cold, icy gaze. She had her right hand on her hip and was shaking her head back and forth disapprovingly.

JAYCEE

Finger fields of sunshine and raspberry kisses, sugar plums growing from lime trees, my world was filled with happy little birdies as I broke it down with my Danny. Turquoise, how did he know about the turquoise? I stopped dancing.

"Danny, I think it might be time for us to paint."

Danny looked at his watch. "We're late. Let's make a run for it. Do you have your tube and brush?" Danny asked.

I looked down at my hands, obviously not. I was dancing.

"No, I think I left them by the sign-up board!" I shouted over the music.

We ran over to the board, and my paint was nowhere in sight.

"We're at canvas number eleven and we're only ten minutes late. Don't worry, we'll get some more paint," Danny assured me.

We skipped over to the canvases, nine, ten, and eleven. Jen was painting orange hearts on our canvas board, and Tiff was painting blue hearts on Jen's skirt, with the turquoise paint that Danny gave me.

"Hey! What are you doing? This is our spot," I asserted.

I looked over to Danny. He wasn't amused by this either.

"Hey, girls, this is supposed to be our time slot. I reserved this easel for us," Danny said nicely.

I walked over to the girls. This was not right. "What's going on? Tiff, that's my paint!" I said.

Tiff laughed a wicked laugh, and her skin shimmer was totally gone. Nowhere to be seen, no color at all. That was very bad.

"What? Jay, I thought the paint was for everyone. Anyway you and Danny are late for your time slot. You snooze, you lose! Hold still Jen," Tiff said, and placed another heart on Jen.

Jen giggled and stood up straight, allowing Tiff to finish.

Danny approached Tiff and Jen. "Girls, I'm really sorry but we signed up for this board. Tiff, if you don't mind, can you please give Jay her paint back?"

Tiff ignored Danny's request. She started to splatter the paint on the canvas. "Paint is for painting, Danny, and you have to learn how to share!" Tiff shouted.

Campers gathered around our canvas. They sensed tension. I was a little nervous. Why was Tiff being so mean to us? I looked around for Lex. I didn't see her anywhere. I felt a wet glob of paint plop on me.

"Cut it out, you're getting paint on us," I advised.

Danny tried to take the paint out of Tiff's hand with no luck.

"No, don't touch my paint!" she shrieked.

Jen continued making her art on the canvas and decided to use the splatter technique as well. I walked toward Jen, hoping that I could stop her, but before I knew it, I was hit from the side with a big clump of orange paint, while Tiff splattered turquoise paint all over the place. A huge glob was in my hair and on my outfit. Orange and blue paint was everywhere.

"Jen, my skirt!" I shouted.

Jen laughed and said, "Jay, you look good in orange."

Tiff chuckled, too, and then everyone was snickering at me. Danny stood there, and he appeared upset and confused. All I saw were lots of campers' faces laughing and pointing at me.

I was so embarrassed and I was dripping with paint. I looked at Danny one last time, and his sweet face was crushed. His eyes begged me to stay, but I couldn't. I needed to get out of there.

I pushed my way through the crowd and heard Danny calling my name. I ran past Craig as he walked to break up the crowd.

"Jay, what's wrong, what happened?" Craig asked, concerned.

How could they have done this to me? I thought we were friends. I yanked the door open and ran out into the fresh air. I breathed in the salty smell of the ocean and hickory wood from the trees. I ran as fast as I could.

CHAPTER 11

ALEXA

I was huffing and puffing. It was hard to keep up with her. "Jay!" I screamed as loud as I could. I looked down at my bare feet. The grass wove in and out of my toes in the moonlight.

"Jay," I hollered again. I saw her hair bouncing up and down ahead of me. Where was she going? "Jay, stop, you're running too fast!" I called out.

Jay looked back, still running. She turned left by the small bridge. I continued to glide through the grass. I couldn't believe Tiff and Jen. I saw the whole thing. I wanted to help but I didn't know what to do.

I spotted her. Jay sat dangling her feet in the koi pond. She squinted in the distance at my silhouette. Tears ran down her face. Harold was with her. His floating, translucent arms were wrapped around her in a hug. I wondered, did she feel him?

"Lex, is that you?" Jay asked, sniffling.

"Yes, it's me. I've been running after you. Didn't you hear me calling your name?" I said, out of breath.

I sat down next to her and dangled my feet in the pond too.

"No, I mean I heard something but my thoughts were running wild. Did you see what they did to me?" Jay cried.

I didn't like to see Jay weep. It always made me sob too.

"Yes, I did. I don't understand, why they did that," I sniffled.

I put my arm around her. I cautiously said, "Harold is here Jay. I thought you should know." Harold looked at me, happy that I mentioned him.

"Oh really, did he see what happened too?"

"Yes, Harold says he saw everything and he doesn't like how Tiff and Jen treated you. He's upset over it too." He embraced Jay some more.

"He's giving you a hug now," I said, leery of how Jay would react to that.

"That's nice. I can use a hug, thank you, Harold," Jay said as she tried to smile.

I didn't think she felt it, but I guessed she was willing to play along.

"You look so pretty tonight, I love your hair like this," Jay said as she twirled one of my locks.

"I don't know. I feel awkward," I shrugged.

Jay laughed a little. "Lex! Stop that right now. You're beautiful!"

I looked down at my toes, not sure about that. I was glad I could distract her thoughts for the moment though.

Jay scratched her head. She stared at me in deep thought. "I don't understand. Why did Tiff and Jen do that? They ruined my outfit and embarrassed me in front of the whole camp," Jay cried.

"I'm sure they feel bad about it, I mean Tiff is your best friend. She's got to know what she did was wrong," I said.

Jay looked up at me as tears streamed down her face. "No, you're my best friend, Lex."

"You're my best friend too."

We hugged and Harold joined us.

"Hey, Harold this is a sisters-only hug!" I giggled.

Jay laughed. "Yeah, Harold, sisters-only."

I was happy Jay had a smile on her face. Jay looked at the pond. "Should we make a wish?" she asked.

"Yes, we should." I smiled and I pulled out a coin from my mini–messenger bag, handed it to Jay, and tried to remember what Celeste said.

We stood up and held hands. "What should we wish for?" I asked Jay.

Jay looked intently at the water. The moonlight hit her face, and her freckles showed a bit. "What I really want is for everyone to be happy and loving, no more fighting and mean girls. Is that possible?"

"I hope so," I said.

"Ready, Lex?"

I nodded.

"Let's think of our wish really hard and repeat the rhyme together on the count of three," Jay directed. "1-2-3..."

A thought, a hope, a wish, a dream.
I ask for help, my fish agleam:
This coin holds my intentions.
Take them through vast dimensions.
Return them here—Camp In-Between.

Jay flicked the coin into the pond. It plopped in the water, creating a beautiful ripple, and the koi darted toward it. We relished the sight. The fish congregated where our coin landed.

"Jay do you see this? Look at all the koi," I said, amazed.

"I know," Jay said, watching. "I think they like our wish," she smiled. "Can I sleep in your bed tonight?"

That was something we frequently did at home. It started as a result of my interrupted sleep, but sometimes we just had sleepovers for fun.

"Sure."

"Let's go, I'm tired," Jay said.

Our coin sparkled from the bottom of the shallow wishing pond. Jay grabbed my hand, Harold grabbed hers, and we walked off in the moonlight back to our bunk.

CHAPTER 12

ALEXA

It was five to nine. Celeste pulled me out of breakfast and walked me over to Think Time. I was so glad I didn't have to play softball with the rest of the bunk. Mom really helped me out by calling the camp.

I've always been a loner. Although I always have Jay, so I guess I'm never really alone. I do have other friends, but everyone thinks they're just imaginary. Jay believes me, she knows they're real. We have always been connected like that. It's one of the things that kept us close.

"Celeste, does Jay know that I am here? I didn't have a chance to tell her at breakfast," I said.

"I'm going over to the softball field after I drop you off, so I will be sure to let her know," Celeste confirmed.

I was concerned about Jay. She was still really shaken up from how Tiff and Jen treated her at the dance party the night before. I thought we should tell Celeste or Mrs. Miller about what happened, but I knew Jay was hesitant to do so. She was still processing what happened. Jay didn't talk to anyone besides me at breakfast that morning. Maybe she would be happier on the softball field.

"Well, here we are, Lex. This is Think Time," Celeste said.

I looked around the open and airy room. There was no furniture, except for shelves stacked with purple and green mats on the wall.

A beautiful girl in her early twenties entered the room. She had auburn shoulder-length straight hair, light brown eyes, and a gentle presence about her.

"Hi Lex, I am Yolanda, your instructor. Let's grab you a mat and get you settled in."

Celeste walked me over to the shelf. I picked out a purple mat, and so did she. I placed it down and unraveled my worry beads. Yolanda and Celeste joined me on the floor.

"Let's get nice and comfy." Yolanda lay on her back, and I followed her lead. "We are going to breathe deep to make sure we are relaxed and let our bodies embrace this tranquil state," Yolanda instructed.

I sat up. I was confused. "I don't understand, when can I use my worry beads?" I asked Celeste.

Yolanda looked at Celeste, perplexed.

Celeste smiled and said, "Yes, we can't forget about the worry beads. Okay Lex, close your eyes and gently roll the worry beads in your hand. Imagine that you are connected to a cord that attaches your body to the ground, kind of like a tree trunk. Concentrate really hard and focus all your energy to the center of your forehead. Try as best you can to clear away your thoughts and be still. Allow yourself to relax and repeat in your head, 'I am safe.'"

I did as Celeste instructed. I told myself, "I am safe, I am safe, I am safe." A few minutes passed by. I was calm. I heard the door softly close shut, and I knew that I was alone.

JAYCEE

"Batter up," Jason, the umpire, called out. I was at bat. Tiff was pitching for the other team. This was awkward. We hadn't spoken to each other all morning. Jen said a few words to me at breakfast, such as "Pass the ketchup," but so far, the girls were ignoring me.

My heart hurt. I inched up to the plate. Tiff was a really good pitcher. We played softball together at home. We always threw the ball back and forth, and I helped her strengthen her arm when we were waiting in between innings. I knew her windmill pitch. It was fast, and I was nervous.

I looked toward the dugout, where my team was lined up watching me at bat. I somehow wound up on Jen's team, after I was picked last. I still couldn't believe that I was chosen at the end. I was the best first baseman ever. I played first base at our middle school, and I was also team captain.

My heart hurt again. Tiff looked at me, icy eyes, no shimmer. She stared me down as she prepared for the pitch. She released the ball. It came flying straight down the middle of the plate. It was perfect, and I just let it pass me by.

"Strike one," Jason announced.

"Hey! I wasn't even ready," I said.

"You were a few inches from the plate Jay. That means ready," he said.

I knew he was right. Tiff wound up for the pitch. The ball was released. I swung. The ball popped up toward the dugout.

"Foul ball, strike two!" Jason called out.

I couldn't strike out, I just couldn't. Tiff smiled. I looked around the field.

Vee-Vee was on first base. She was the only one who was nice to me that morning.

I glanced over toward the dugout again. The girls looked mean. Their shimmers were dark and muddy. That was never a good sign. They were my teammates, so why did I sense they wanted me to strike out? I stepped toward the plate. Jen stood up and started a cheer.

Jay-cee, what a floozy.
She thinks she's all that,
Because she spoke to Danny.
Jay, Jay go away,
You've lost your friends, anyway.

Laughs. Celeste quieted them down, but it was too late. My eyes got misty. Tiff smiled and wound up for the pitch. Why were they doing this to me?

The ball was released. I swung with all my might, making contact. The ball flew off into the outfield. I ran as fast as I could.

CHAPTER 13

ALEXA

I was in a relaxed state. I pictured my body connected to the Earth attached by a cord. I felt as light as a feather. My limbs were loose. I gave into the jellylike sensation.

Bang! There was a loud noise. I was immediately pulled out of my tranquil state. I thought someone had opened the door. I rubbed my eyes. The room was dark, and I didn't think Yolanda was near.

"Lex? Lex are you here?"

I knew that voice, but her tone was desolate and timid, not her outgoing spunky self.

I sat up. "Jay, is that you?"

"Yes, it's me. Where are you, Lex? It's so dark in here. Where are the lights?"

I turned on the lights. Jay was standing in front of me. Her golden hair was covered in mud, and she was hysterically crying to the point that she could barely talk. She gasped for breaths in between sobs and sat next to me.

"Jay, what's wrong?" I asked.

She didn't answer, but it was okay, she didn't have to. I embraced her in a hug.

"What happened at softball? Did Tiff do something mean again? Did you fall on your way over here?"

Jay shook her head. "No, Lex, no, much worse, like one of the worst things ever."

I kept holding and rubbing her hand. "Okay Jay, just tell me what happened.

Jay looked at me. "All the girls hate me. First it all started when Jen and Tiff were picked to be captains and chose players for each team. No one picked me until the very end. I was the last pick! Can you believe that?"

She pulled some mud off from her hair. "Look at my hair! Tiff was pitching, and I got a home run. Tiff tried to block me as I approached home base." Jay sniffled and continued. "She had a fistful of mud and threw it on me as I crossed the plate. It landed all over me before I could even get in safely, and all the girls were laughing."

"I think she got in trouble but I don't know, because I just made a run for it. When I left, they were saying this awful cheer about me." Jay stumbled trying to remember how it went.

Jay-cee, what a floozy.
She thinks she's all that,
Because she spoke to Danny.
Jay, Jay go away.
You've lost your friends, anyway.

"Really, they said that?" I asked. I couldn't believe they would do that to Jay. After all, they were her best friends.

"Yes, can you believe that? And the chant was led by Jen!" she cried.

Thud, loud bang. The front door opened and shut again.

"Lex? Are you here?"

"It's Mrs. Miller," I whispered to Jay.

"Yes, hi, Mrs. Miller. I am over here in the corner, by the fan."

Jay quickly wiped away her tears.

"Oh Jay, hi. What a surprise...." She took a second look, confused. "Jay? What is in your hair? Is that mud?" Mrs. Miller scrunched her face.

Uh-oh. Jay looked uncomfortable.

I quickly said, "Um, yeah. Jay slid in the mud during softball."

Knowing Jay, I doubted she wanted to talk about what really happened. Jay nodded her head, agreeing with my story.

Mrs. Miller seemed very distracted. I was afraid Jay would get in trouble for being there with me, but I guessed Mrs. Miller was okay with it.

"Well, I am glad you are together. Where's Yolanda?" Mrs. Miller asked with an annoyed look on her face. I assumed that she thought Yolanda was slacking off.

Mrs. Miller continued, "Well anyway, first things first. Listen girls, I just got a phone call from your Mom. She needs you both to call her right away. It's important. I am going to take you to the camp office so you can use my phone, okay?"

Jay and I just looked at each other and nodded.

"Sure," I said. Uh-oh. Something's wrong. I felt a knot in my stomach.

Mrs. Miller took us through the rec hall's long corridor to the camp office. She guided us to a room in the very back of the building.

"Please girls, have a seat," Mrs. Miller said, pointing to the two oversized chairs across from her desk. She picked up the phone. "I'm going to leave the room so you girls can have your privacy, but when you're done, please open the door and I'll come back in."

"Okay," I said.

Mrs. Miller dialed our Mom's number and handed me the phone. She walked out and closed the door.

"Hello?" Mom said.

"Hi, Mom," Jay and I said simultaneously.

"Hi, girls," Mom said, sobbing. We knew it. She couldn't hide the sound of her sniffles from us. I could visualize the tears falling down her face.

"How are my girls?" Mom asked, trying to conceal her sadness.

"Mom, what's wrong? What is it?" I asked gently.

"I am sorry to have to tell you this and ruin all your fun at camp, but, it's about Grandma."

"Grandma?" Jay and I gasped nervously.

"Is she still in the hospital?" Jay asked.

"Not exactly, I don't know how else to say this ... but Grandma is no longer with us. She passed on." Mom cried into the phone. "I am so sorry, girls, to have to give you this type of news."

"Oh no," said Jay. "Grandma is gone?"

Tears flowed down our faces. We knew what this meant. No more Grandma. No more Grandma's chicken soup. No more sweet smell of her Grandma scent.

"We are still figuring things out. It just happened last night. Listen girls, I know this is upsetting and sad, but for what it's worth, please try to continue on as best you can with camp. There was nothing any of us could have done. Grandma had a really long and full life. She is at peace now. She loved you girls so much," Mom said reassuringly.

Jay and I sat hunched over crying in Mrs. Miller's chair. I sobbed loudly, so did Jay.

Jay stuttered, trying to speak, "O-k-a-y Mom."

Jay and I were speechless. It was the first time both of us experienced a loss.

"Dad and I will come pick you girls up so you can say your good-byes. But right now, please, try as best you can to continue on. I will call the camp later once we have everything sorted out," Mom instructed us.

"Okay, call us later," I said, concerned.

"Yes, of course. I love you girls. I'll be in touch soon," Mom said softly and hung up the phone.

Jay and I held each other tight. We were so sad and confused. I looked over at the window and saw the beautiful butterfly from last night fluttering its wings, perched on Mrs. Miller's windowsill. I took in the moment and kept it to myself. I made a mental note.

Jay got up from her chair and opened the door while tears streamed down her face. Mrs. Miller walked in. She looked at us both and crouched down, giving us a big warm hug.

"I'm so sorry girls. Is there anything that I can do to make you feel better?" Mrs. Miller asked.

I grasped onto Mrs. Miller's embrace and thrust all my sadness into her arms. Jay rubbed her face, wiping some of her tears away.

I stared at the windowsill. The butterfly was gone, and I was in deep thought, trying to remember my dream from last night. I thought hard and it came to me. I suddenly remembered the image. Grandma visited me. She was there at camp, and she was tucking Jay and me into bed because we had a sleepover. I woke up remembering her words: "Sleep well, my sweet little dumplings." It had been so vivid and real. Could she have really been with us?

Just then, Mrs. Miller said, "I know you've been through a lot today. Would you girls like to take some time before rejoining the rest of your bunk? Maybe we can watch a movie?"

I wanted to be alone with Jay. Jay looked at me, almost as if she could read my thoughts and answered for us. "I think we would like to be alone.... Maybe we can go to Think Time, and rest instead?"

"I'd like that too," I said.

Mrs. Miller paused momentarily and replied, "Yes, of course you can. I will sit with you girls and make sure that you are okay."

As Mrs. Miller walked us down the hall to Think Time, I watched Jay touch her muddy hair in disgust. I didn't know if it was the right time to bring it up, but I knew Jay was distressed. "Mrs. Miller, I think Jay has something else to tell you," I said.

Jay glanced at me, and I nodded, indicating for her to go ahead.

Mrs. Miller looked at Jay and asked, "What is it, Jay? You can tell me anything."

Jay diverted her eyes to the floor and then back to meet Mrs. Miller's gaze. "Well, I don't know what to say but I feel bad and sad, not just about Grandma but about the girls in our bunk," Jay said.

Mrs. Miller grabbed Jay's hand. Jay felt the mud in her hair again, and tears trickled down her face.

"Please go on Jay, I'm listening and want to help you."

Jay hesitated and then continued. "The girls in our bunk are being really mean. They're calling me names, they threw mud on my hair and are ganging up on me."

Mrs. Miller looked at Jay and said genuinely, "I am really sorry this happened. You did the right thing by telling me. Don't worry, I can assure you both that I am going to handle this. You girls just go ahead and try to relax."

JAYCEE

I took a green mat and placed it beside Lex's purple one. We lay down next to each other.

"I miss Grandma," I said.

"Me too," Lex confirmed.

"Do you think Grandma knows how sad we are and how much we miss her?" I asked Lex.

Lex was silent. That was odd, she's usually good at comforting me. I turned my head and looked at her. She wasn't listening to me. Her eyes were closed, and she looked like she was in some deep trance. What was she doing?

Lex's eyes shot open, and she said, "I see Grandma. Harold is trying to communicate with me. It's Grandma, I see her, and she's waiting for us on the mountain trail. Is that right, Harold? Is she there?" Lex asked.

"What? I'm confused," I told Lex.

"She's in the mountains? Let me get this straight, our Grandma is in the mountains, like *our* mountains? Is that what you see Lex?"

Lex was excited. "Yes, I see her Jay! She is in the mountains overlooking the camp. Yep, Harold is here next to me, and he says it's true, and I believe him," Lex advised me confidently.

At that point, if she was convinced, then so was I.

"Well then let's go find her right away. Should we pack a bag?" I asked.

"We can use the food in the package we just received from Mom, the granola bars, nuts, and dried fruit, you know, so we don't starve," Lex directed.

"Yes, of course! We can drink from the river. I don't know if there *is* a river, but I'm sure we'll find one. We can go through the woods behind our bunk. I just hope we don't get caught.

Lex looked at her watch. "It's free swim."

"Perfect, okay so let's –"

"Shh!" Lex hushed me up.

Mrs. Miller and Yolanda were headed back toward us.

"Okay, girls, you'll be in good hands with Yolanda. I'll be back later to see how you're doing," Mrs. Miller called out.

Yolanda greeted Jay and looked at us warmly. "I am so sorry girls. I know this must be really hard. You can relax in here as long as you want. Can I get you anything?" Yolanda asked.

Lex and I shook our heads.

Yolanda handed us pillows and blankets from the closet.

"Thanks," Lex said as she took them from Yolanda's hands.

Lex looked at me and smirked. We were likely thinking the very same thing. This was perfect for our escape plan.

"Okay, thanks. We're pretty tired. I think we'll take a nap," I said, trying not to sound too enthusiastic.

"You girls get all nice and comfy. I'll give you some privacy. I will be in my office, if you need me," Yolanda advised.

Yolanda left the room, and Lex and I were alone. We were stoked. We waited a few minutes in silence, until the coast was clear. We gently opened the door and snuck out.

CHAPTER 14

ALEXA

I ran over to my bed and took out a big cardboard box. Puzzles, stickers, and sudoku came flying out. There it was, my large plastic bag filled with snacks.

I took out my small backpack and threw the food in along with my book, a flashlight, glasses, sweatpants, and sweatshirt for at night, when it was sure to be cold.

Jay was over at her bed, doing the same. I ran toward her and gestured that it was time to go.

We walked behind the bunk toward a large wooded trail.

"Jay, look, a butterfly. It's not just any butterfly, it's the same one that I saw two times before."

"She's so pretty," Jay said. "Look at her wings, she's a mix of our favorite colors, purple and blue."

"I think she likes us. We should give her a name," I said.

"Okay, how about Rainbow?" Jay asked.

"No, she's not a Rainbow. How about Indigo? The color of her beautiful wings," I declared.

Jay smiled, satisfied with the name. Indigo was waiting for us a little further down the path. She was fluttering around us as if she liked the name too.

"I think Indigo wants us to follow her," Jay called out.

"Okay Indigo, you lead the way, off to the mountains we go," I proclaimed.

JAYCEE

Skipping and running and laughing – what an adventure! We were off to find Grandma. Lex was smiling and giggling as her eyes were fixed on Indigo. She was convinced that we were on the right path. I believed Lex. She had never been wrong before. A few hundred yards away I saw a large wooden gate. It was locked. I jumped on it. I looked down. Lex was not following.

"C'mon Lex, don't be scared, just follow me." My feet were dangling around the planks of the gate. I leaped off and landed on the other side.

"Jay, I am afraid," Lex admitted. "It's so high, I don't think that I can do this."

"Lex, it's really not hard at all." The gate wasn't more than five feet tall. "You can do it," I encouraged her.

We had to get a move on. We were only at the outskirts of camp.

"Lex, now!" I hollered.

"Okay, I'm coming!" she retorted.

Lex grabbed onto the gate and mustered her body up and over its pickets. She jumped and brushed off the dirt that clung to her knees.

"Phew, I am glad we got that over with. Which way should we go?" Lex asked. She was looking at Indigo. Our little butterfly was leading the way.

We were in the thick of the mountains. There was lush greenery all around us. The air was crisp, and the mountain peaks were so high they looked like they touched the sky.

We hiked up a very steep trail. The ledges were unfenced. As I looked down at the humungous drop, I knew that it was just a small matter of time before Lex freaked out. I was about to panic too. I felt a lump well up in my throat. I swallowed and took a deep breath.

I started our favorite cheer, to keep us distracted from the height.

Red as the roses that sprout from the ground.
Yellow, so yellow, the sun it shines down.
Orange is sweetness that grows on the trees.
Green is for goodness, the earth and the leaves.
Blue is the sky, and it's deep as the sea.
Purple, so vibrant and pure as can be.
The rainbow of colors surrounds you and me.

Lex sang the verse again, and we repeated it twice more.

The singing worked. It helped move us through the steepest part of the trail. The terrain became flat and grassy. Lex stopped walking and started to whine.

"I'm hungry," she said.

I was getting tired too. We had hiked up the trail for such a long time. Lex moved off the path and sat on a large boulder. She opened her backpack and took out a bag of dried apricots. I heard her munching on them. She reached out and handed me some.

It was the first smile on her face I'd seen that day. I took the apricot. In that moment, for a brief second or two, we both forgot the pain the day had brought us.

ALEXA

I jumped off the big boulder that I was using for a seat. "I just want to tie my shoes, and then we can go," I called out to Jay.

I bent down and grabbed my pink laces while Jay turned the other way, holding her phone in the air to see if she could get a bar or two.

A large gust of wind nearly knocked me off my feet. The leaves on the trees swayed, and dirt lifted from the ground. It was a big gust. Rabbits, squirrels, lizards, and other forest animals of all sorts quickly scurried past me.

"Jay, I'm a little scared, I have this weird feeling."

Jay's eyes widened. As fast as the gust came in, it was gone. It was eerily quiet. "What was that?" I asked.

Indigo was frantic and touching our heads while she bopped up and down. She wanted us to follow her.

"Okay, Indigo. Lex, let's go, this is getting a little weird," Jay said.

"Where are we going?" I asked.

"Well, we can't just stay here," Jay replied.

We followed Indigo's lead, and she brought us to a dirt-covered cave.

"I don't like caves, they scare me," I said.

Indigo fluttered by the entrance, urging us to go in. All the animals rushed into the cave ahead of us.

"I don't know about this, Jay. It's so dark in there," I said.

"Let's just see what it is," Jay insisted.

The entrance to the cave was about the same size as us. Jay opened up my sack and took out the flashlight. We turned it on and walked in, but the cave was already glowing with light.

"Wow, it's so bright, I guess we don't need this," Jay said as she turned off the flashlight.

The glow started to dissipate, and we saw a figure. A person, but not a person at all. We heard the words, "Don't be scared, girls," called out to us.

"Who are you, what is this?" Jay blurted out.

A little pink man about four feet tall shined through the light in front of us. All the animals we saw scamper in the cave lovingly surrounded him. Bunnies, snakes, lizards, stray cats, birds, and Indigo flocked to his side.

"His skin shimmers a blue hue. It matches Indigo's wings," Jay whispered into my ear.

He had a big head and big almond-shaped green eyes. His body was small and skinny. His voice was sweet and inviting.

"Welcome, Lex and Jay, I have been waiting for you," he said.

CHAPTER 15

JAYCEE

I screamed. It was so not like me to be scared, but I was. "What is it? Who is it?" I asked Lex.

"How does he know our names?" Lex asked.

"It looks like a Martian that you see in the movies," I said.

Lex looked at me. "I think he's kind of cute," she shrugged.

How was she smiling and giggling like this was no big deal? She's the one who was always scared.

I pulled her arm, but she didn't budge as the Martian approached me.

"Hey! Take one more step and I'll scream again!" I announced.

I stepped back and inched closer to Lex and said, "I think we should go."

"No, don't leave," he said.

He had heard me! He waved his hand in the air, and gold glitter glistened all around us.

"Glitter? What are you, a magician?" I asked.

He suddenly disappeared. We looked around.

"Hey, where'd you go?" I asked.

"I'm over here," he said.

We turned our heads. "Where?" I asked.

He appeared in front of us. "Surprise," he laughed. Lex was laughing. He disappeared again. The birds in the cave came together and flew him around the room. Lex was enchanted by his magic, but I wasn't amused.

"Jay, don't be scared, I am here to help you and Lex." He opened up his hands and released something in the air. The air got calmer.

"Jay, chill out," he said.

I mouthed to Lex, "chill out?" A little pink man just told me to chill?

He smiled and brushed his shoulders off, just like I always did. "Yeah, you heard me. You're being kind of lame. I expected more from the sister with the big imagination."

He took a step toward me, and I didn't back away. My curious spirit awakened.

"Okay, little pink man, go ahead and make your case," I said with my arms crossed.

"Well, I am a little pink man, you're right about that. My name is Artie. I'm not a Martian at all, well, I'm not human either...," he trailed off.

I wondered how he got there and why he wanted to see us.

Artie suddenly responded to my thoughts. "Jay, I know you and Lex pretty well, as you will soon be assured, and I traveled a long journey to see you. I am here to take you on a very special mission that only a few people get to experience."

Was this really happening? How was he reading my mind?

"I am telepathic," Artie answered.

I had to digest the whole reading thoughts part. Was I in a dream? I questioned.

"No, Jay, this is really happening. It's not your imagination. I come from Arcturus. Well actually, more specifically, I come from a dimensional plane that exists within the outer atmosphere of Arcturus – but we call that Arcturus too. We, Arcturians, are one of the most advanced civilizations in the galaxy."

"Hey, that's the name of our bunk!" Lex called out.

"Yes, I know, and that's not happanstance. There are no coincidences. We put you in that bunk for a reason," Artie said.

"We?" I questioned.

"Jay, I want you to know I saw what those girls did to you today. They are bullying you, and that's not okay," Artie stated.

"How did he know that?" I asked Lex.

"Like I said before, I am telepathic, that's all," Artie stated confidently.

He disappeared. He reappeared hanging upside down from the ceiling. Ha! We giggled. He was kind of funny.

"I see and know all, you'll see. Don't worry, girls, you are in good hands with me," Artie informed us.

He bounced back down from the ceiling and grabbed our hands. Before we knew it, we were hanging upside down from the ceiling with him.

"Oh my goodness, this is so cool," Lex said. She was enjoying this.

"How did you do that?" Lex asked.

"It's all up here," Artie pointed to his head. "Soon you'll be able to do the same thing."

"What? No way!" I said.

"Way," he replied.

"Okay, I'll believe it when I see it, Marty Artie," I said sarcastically.

"You said you know us, how?" Lex asked. He floated us down gently to the ground, and we landed on our feet.

"I'm no stranger to you girls, I've been with you since you were born. Ask Harold, I think he'll know," Artie suggested.

"Harold!" Lex gasped.

"How do you know about Harold?" I asked.

Artie started to walk on the walls of the cave.

"What is he doing? He's so bizarre," I told Lex.

"C'mon girls, lighten up. Have some fun," Artie suggested.

The cave filled up with red, blue, yellow, and green balloons. I was not amused. I was still skeptical of our new friend.

"Harold?" I said cautiously. I turned to Lex, who was grouping balloons in her hands.

"Lex, can you speak to Harold and ask him if he approves of this whole thing or whatever is going on here?"

I was nervous. I knew I was because I was biting my nails. How was I supposed to believe a pink Martian man anyway?

CHAPTER 16

ALEXA

"Harold, Harold are you there?" I asked.

We waited. Silence. "Hmm … he is not appearing right away, let me try again. Oh good, there you are," I said.

Before I could even ask Harold the question he had a response. I listened to Harold's message.

"Jay, Harold says that Artie is here to help us find Grandma and that he is a good galactic person. Harold also said that he thinks you need to relax," I informed.

"I bet you added that last part," Jay said sarcastically.

"No, not at all," I replied.

Jay's worried face turned from a frown into a smile. "You are cute, Marty," she said.

"Artie," he corrected her.

I thought Jay was beginning to like him after all.

"Artie, if you're a galactic person, where's your spaceship?" Jay inquired.

"I don't need a spaceship. I travel with my mind," Artie said, smiling at us.

I started to fidget. I wished I could sit down; climbing through the mountains had made me tired. Just then, out of thin air, a lush velvet sofa and table appeared behind us. On the table was a pitcher full of lemonade. It looked delicious, and I was thirsty.

"I thought you might be," Artie said.

My mouth dropped open in astonishment. Holy cow, how cool was this, he really *could* read minds. Okay, I was convinced, I thought to myself.

"Thank you, Lex, I appreciate that," Artie replied to my thoughts.

"What else can you do?" Jay asked.

"I am here to show you where you are really from, my little star seeds," Artie stated.

"Star seeds?" Jay questioned.

"Yes, you've been planted here by me and your galactic family," Artie said.

"By you?" Jay repeated. "What do you mean? Galactic family? Mom and Dad know you?"

"Not quite, my little seedlings. This is why I am here, to take you to Arcturus with me."

"Wait a minute, wait just a minute. Who said we are going anywhere with you. C'mon, Lex, let's get out of here," Jay directed.

Just as Jay began to get up from the couch, Artie joined us. He sat in the middle and started pouring us cups of lemonade.

"Yum, this is the best lemonade I've ever had," I said.

Artie manifested his own glassful of a royal blue liquid. It was glowing.

"Wow, what's that?" Jay asked.

"It's my Vigor," Artie responded.

Artie guzzled it down and continued: "I know what happened to your Grandma, and I want you to know that she is safe. I am going to take you to find her."

I knew she was looking for us! "See Jay, I told you," I said proudly. "I saw an image of her in the mountains. That's why Jay and I are here. Can I try your Vigor, Artie, please?" I begged.

"Sorry, Lex, not yet. You don't have the powers yet to absorb this juice. If you drink it now, it may make you feel sick," Artie advised.

Jay rolled her eyes and said, "You're going to take us to our Grandma? We know what happened, she's not coming back."

Artie gently patted Jay on the back and said, "Just trust me. I hope you will. I am here to help you two. I know this all sounds strange right now, but please just believe me. You are gifted with special talents, and I am just here to show you how to use your powers on Earth."

I think the power part piqued Jay's curiosity.

"Well, if you're for real, how do we get these powers anyway?" Jay asked.

Artie held out his hands and, poof, two beautiful, purple crystal necklaces appeared in his grasp.

Their beauty mesmerized me. Jay's eyes sparkled with intrigue.

"These are Arcturian Amethysts," Artie stated. "One is for you, and the other is for Lex. You will need these from now on."

Artie's fingers glowed with light as he held the necklaces in his hands and closed his eyes.

"What are you doing?" I asked.

"I'm filling your necklaces up with energy. I am connecting with Arcturus and the Earth so I can provide you with the tools you need. There, all done," Artie declared.

Poof! The amethysts appeared around our necks like magic.

"Wow," Jay said, admiring her necklace. "It's so pretty."

"If you come with me to Arcturus, I will show you what this is all about. How about it, girls? Are we ready to travel through the astral planes?" Artie asked.

I turned to my left side and waited. Harold appeared on cue. He was nodding his head and told me that it was okay to go. I looked over at Jay and said, "Jay, Harold says, we can go with Artie."

Jay paused and asked, "Can we bring our necklaces there?"

"Yes, as I said, you will need them. You will use them visiting Arcturus as well as on Earth," Artie assured us.

Jay smiled wide and said, "Okay, you've convinced me. But I have my eye on you, little guy. Let's do it, Lex, are you in?"

"Yes, I am in. Let the traveling begin."

Artie took our hands, and we walked to a designated spot in the middle of the cave. We sat on the dirt floor.

"When we sit on the ground, we are connected to the Earth. Holding hands transmits my energy to you. Close your eyes and imagine that you are connected to a cord that attaches your body to the ground, kind of like a tree trunk. Focus all your energy on being attached to the cord and repeat this verse three times with me," Artie instructed.

We are going up up,
And far far away,
To a land full of love.
Our gifts ready to make use of.
Our minds filled with intention.
Take us to a higher dimension.

"Ready, 1, 2, 3," Artie directed. We said the verse three times. A big warm gust of air surrounded us, and we were moving fast.

Swoosh, the air sucked us up, and away we went, into the universe. It felt like we had been traveling for only a few seconds and then, thump! It was calm and still.

"Okay girls, we have arrived, you can open your eyes, my little star seeds," Artie instructed.

We opened our eyes and waited for our bodies to reconnect. We were no longer on Earth. Arcturus welcomed us.

CHAPTER 17

JAYCEE

I sure hoped Harold was right when he told Lex that it was okay to go on this adventure. We were somewhere very far away, and I felt weird and out of sorts. My body was tingly, and my vision was blurry. I rubbed my eyes repeatedly, but everything looked pixelated.

"Lex, where are you? Can you see me?" I asked.

"Sort of, but, everything is hazy," Lex answered.

"Girls, grab onto my hand," Artie suggested.

I heard Artie's gentle voice, and I felt my way around to get closer to him.

"We're here, star seeds. This is Arcturus, your ancient home. You are back and should be adapting very soon. Here, drink some Vigor. It will fill you up with instant energy and help you adjust," Artie informed us.

Artie squeezed our hands tighter and walked us over to some sort of blue liquid fountain. Our vision was returning. I squinted for extra clarity.

Lex touched the fountain and guided her way around its spout. "Is it okay to drink this now, Artie?" she asked.

"Yes, you need this. You are in another dimension many years more evolved than planet Earth."

Lex hesitated.

"I'll try it first," I told her. I leaned in and took a big slurp. Oh wow, we must've really been in some kind of amazing universe because I was drinking a chocolate milkshake from a fountain. "Chocolate milkshakes are my favorite! I'm never going back home," I said loudly.

"My turn," Lex said. I moved away and Lex leaned in and took a long sip. "Chocolate? The Vigor tastes like blueberries and raspberries, yum! It's so delicious, I want more," Lex said.

The Vigor worked. My vision was back, and the tingling was gone. I felt alert and alive. This place was radiating with vibrant life. I wondered if it was the Vigor or just being there, but I had boundless energy.

"Artie, this place is magnificent, it's like a fantasy land," I said, surprised. I scanned our surroundings. The sky was a pearly pink, and there were gigantic purple mountains everywhere. I looked down and there was no grass; instead the ground was filled with cushiony white clouds. I took a step on the ground and could bounce up and down.

"Whee!" I said as I leaped.

"Look, Lex over there, there are royal blue liquid fountains everywhere," I said.

"I am glad you approve, Jay!" Artie said. "Yes, the fountains give us our energy boosts. It's Vigor Juice," Artie explained.

"Is this the same juice you drank in the cave?" Lex asked.

Artie responded, "Yes, that's it, Lex. You see, the fountains here are endless. They supply us with extra doses of energy. We don't really need it because we ingest energy from the air, but it tastes so good that we can't resist. You can create any flavor you desire with your mind."

Create any flavor with our minds? Oh that must have explained why my first gulp tasted like a chocolate milkshake and Lex's had been a raspberry blueberry juice.

"I want to try again. I would like to create a pineapple mango juice," Lex requested.

Lex leaned in again and slurped up more Vigor. I did the same, obviously keeping my desire for more chocolate milkshake. I looked up, licked away the remaining chocolate goodness on my upper lip, and noticed that there were unusual-looking animals everywhere. They were walking, crawling, and inching toward us.

"Whoa, what's going on, Artie? What's with all the animals?" I asked.

They kept coming closer to us. There must have been hundreds and hundreds of these animals that I had never seen before. They were staring at us as we took each and every step.

"These are our Creations. We rarely ever have Earthling visitors here. They are just watching, that's all," Artie stated.

"Creations? You mean animals?" I suggested.

"No, I mean Creations. Creations are animals here. They are our companions. They are much more advanced than the animals you have on Earth," Artie corrected.

"Oooh, they're so cute and they look so unique," I said as we walked closer to the Creations.

I spotted a fuzzy little koala-like head sticking out from behind a purple palm tree. He peeked out, and I caught his glance. He quickly disappeared again.

I snuck off toward the tree. Intrigued, I gently approached him. He was so preoccupied hiding that I startled him. "Gotcha," I said excitedly as I tagged him on the shoulder.

I had never seen anything quite like him. He looked like a koala, but I knew he wasn't. He had big bulging circular eyes that protruded out of his face and were warm with love. He had a potbelly stomach and a thick, warm, fluffy blue coat of fur. He was as small as a rabbit.

He gasped and quickly scrunched into a ball, wrapping his arms around his head trying to hide. I waited for him to look up.

"I can still see you," I said with a laugh.

He opened his eyes and shook out his blue fur. "I know. It's just ... I wasn't ready to say hello," he said.

"You speak!" I said, amazed.

I couldn't contain my excitement. He was so cute I wanted to pick him up. I started jumping up and down with exhilaration.

The creature smiled and bounced up and down with me. He was eager to speak to me, too.

"Izzy, Izzy, Izzy!"

"Izzy?" I asked.

"Yup that's me," he said in the most adorable high-pitched voice.

I looked closely at Izzy and gently pinched him.

"Ouch, what did you do that for?" he asked.

"I just want to make sure you are real, that's all."

Izzy pinched me back.

"Ouch!" I said.

"Well, you did it first. I'm Izzy, and this is my tree. Would you like to sit with me?"

"Sure, but what exactly are you? I've never seen an animal quite like you."

"Of course not. We only exist on Arcturus. I am a blend, a cross between, as you Earthlings know it, a koala and a chipmunk. A Kochump," Izzy continued. "Creations are hybrid animals. We can think and understand all human thoughts."

"A Kochump?" I questioned. I had never heard of anything like that. "You are so adorable. Why are you hiding behind this tree, Izzy?" I asked.

"Well, I saw you girls coming and I've never seen humans before, that's all."

"Oh Izzy! I have a fantastic idea. Come back to Earth with us so I can show you to all my friends. Please say yes?" I asked.

Lex and Artie had come to my side. Artie didn't look too happy with my proposal to Izzy.

"This is so cool. He talks. I am freaking out. I want a Kochump," I said.

"Jay I don't think that's a good idea...," Lex said nervously.

"Izzy on Earth! Izzy on Earth!" Izzy shrieked with excitement. He jumped up and down and I joined him.

"Izzy wants to come to Earth," I said proudly.

Artie chimed in, "No, no, no. We need Izzy here, Jay. Creations do not leave the Arcturian plane. We have thousands of different animal species here. There's a Cabbit, which is a hybrid of a cat and a rabbit. Here's a Zeeger, a blend of a tiger and a zebra, just to name a few."

I looked around and was amazed at all the different new varieties of animals that surrounded us. As each animal greeted us, I couldn't help but feel the love on the star. It was magnanimous. I looked at Izzy, my tiny little buddy, who was hugging my leg. He climbed up my body and sat on my shoulder.

"Izzy on Earth," he whispered in my ear.

I gave him a wink and petted his head gently. "Izzy on Earth," I said in agreement.

Lex was looking around soaking in all the Creations and majestic scenery. She was getting that look on her face though, uh-oh. Lex was doing that thing she did when she was concerned: rubbing her cheeks up and down with both hands.

"Artie, this place is truly special indeed, but I thought that we would find Grandma here, where is she? How are we ever going to get back to Earth? Besides, won't Mrs. Miller, Celeste, and Mom be worried about us? How will anyone know where we are?" Lex asked nervously.

Lex was going on and on. I knew that tone in Lex's voice; she was anxious. She was getting herself into a big tizzy. Sometimes I wished she didn't worry so much.

"Lex, stop it! It will be okay, right, Artie?" I said reassuringly.

"Why of course, you girls are safe here, and you'll be back to Earth before you know it. Arcturian time and space are a bit different. First you need to learn a few things, and don't worry about Grandma: I'm up to the task and I will keep my promise," Artie said.

"Hey! Where'd Izzy go?" I said, alarmed that my new friend had disappeared. "He didn't even say good-bye."

"Don't worry Jay, I think Izzy is one step ahead of us. He knows where we are headed next," Artie advised.

Artie led us to a white walkway that was as buoyant as a trampoline. As soon as I took my first step, I noticed that my feet were illuminating shades of purple.

"Jay, look at my steps," Lex called out in disbelief as she bounced up and down. "I can see all different shades of purple ... indigo, orchid, plum, and heliotrope." Lex was so excited that she was speaking so fast.

"Yes, I see it too," I confirmed. I took huge leaps in the air. "This is so much fun. I love it here already. Maybe we can stay, indefinitely."

Once Lex settled in, and stopped worrying about back home, she was going to love it here too, because she loved rainbows and colors more than anyone I knew.

I looked down at my feet and saw the various shades of purple. I observed Artie's steps and noticed his steps were forming all different colors. How could that be? Artie's feet were illuminating rays of red, orange, yellow, green, blue, violet, and purple.

Hey, no fair Artie, I thought. I wondered how Artie's steps were forming rainbows and ours were only shades of purple? How was the pathway doing that?

"We are creating these colors by our own energy," Artie responded.

"Artie, how are you able to read my mind like this?" I asked.

"I told you girls, I am telepathic; and now that you are here on the Arcturian plane, so are you. We don't have to speak with our mouths. We send messages through our minds. It has a name. We call it '*menting.*' Try it, girls."

"*Menting*?" Lex questioned.

"Yes, Lex, *menting*," Artie repeated. "Try it, just think to yourself, and we can read your mind."

"Really? Lex, let's try and *ment*," I said curiously. I closed my eyes and thought to myself, "How is our energy creating these shades of purple?"

"Yes, good question, Jay," Lex *mented*.

I could hear Lex answer me. This was the coolest thing ever. We didn't even have to open our mouths. We just *mented!*

"How were we making these purple rainbows? They were so pretty and they followed me everywhere I went!" I *mented*.

"Oh girls, you will soon see, I can't explain everything to you right away. Come on, follow me. I want to show you something," Artie instructed, and he bounced ahead of us.

CHAPTER 18

ALEXA

I calmed down with every step on the walkway and watched my feet continue to form shades of purple. Artie led us off the path to a large glass pyramid. It looked like a giant greenhouse, but it was much more complex.

"What's in here, Artie?" I *mented*.

"This, my friends, is the Creation Station."

"Creation Station, what's that?" Jay *mented*.

"It's the place where we make Creations," Artie responded.

"You make them? You mean they don't...?" I was cut off by Artie's thoughts.

"Yes, Lex, they are able to reproduce on their own, but we can also assist with the population. For example if we notice that there are more Zeegers than Cabbits, we can make more Cabbits if we want to."

"No way! Can you make us one, Artie?" Jay requested.

"I am afraid not, it doesn't work quite like that. Girls, come in, come in. Let's have a look inside," Artie directed.

We walked inside the immense glass structure and saw our new little blue koala-like friend.

"Izzy, you're here," Jay announced joyously.

Izzy was by our side. Smart little guy. Everything was so bright, and the warm sunlight felt pleasant against my skin. I just wanted to soak it all in.

Artie led us to the center of the main room.

"Artie, is this what I think it is?" I *mented*.

Artie *mented* back, "Yes, Lex you are correct, this is where the Creations are bred, and we keep them here until they are ready to enter our atmosphere. The process usually takes about six months or so."

I saw all the baby Creations snuggled in warm, cozy orange blankets. They were so adorable.

"What do you think would happen if I took one home?" Jay asked me.

"No, Jay, don't," I responded adamantly.

Artie approached Jay and said, "No way!"

"But, I want that one ... someday." Jay pointed to one of the Creations.

"Hey, I thought Izzy was coming with you?" Izzy said, referring to himself.

Jay kissed Izzy on the cheek. "Yes, of course my little Izzy bear. I'm sorry, I thought you might want a friend."

"No, Jay. No Creations on Earth," Artie insisted. "This little guy over here, is one of our new Creations," Artie *mented*. "We are trying out this hybrid. It's a cross between a bush baby and a squirrel monkey. We call it a Buskey."

"Trying out?" Jay asked.

"Yes, we try out new blends here too," Artie told us. "We *ment* them with a Rhyme Chime."

"Rhyme Chime!" Izzy echoed.

"A Rhyme Chime...." I *mented*.

"Yes, each Rhyme Chime has a code that is unlocked with the right combination of words. You've seen a Rhyme Chime before, that's how we got here remember?"

"Oh, yes, I remember that," Jay confirmed.

"This shall be a very special trip for you girls indeed," Artie *mented* and grabbed our hands, leading us out the doors and back to the white bouncy path.

CHAPTER 19

JAYCEE

"Izzy, Izzy, where are you?" I *mented*.

"Izzy's a quick one, Jay, come along. We have lots to do and see, Arcturians to meet and places to be," Artie said, ushering me along.

"When I say Jay, you say Lex." I led a cheer because I was just so happy there.

Artie started wiggling his hips as we bounced down the path together. We bounced by hilltops filled with roses, tulips, sunflowers, and petunias.

Artie waved as other Arcturians looked on and stared intently at us. "Don't worry, girls, you'll meet everyone really soon."

The Arcturians were gathered, watching from the steps of their reddish-orange-colored homes.

We continued along the path reciting the cheer. Lex and I bounced around and around, up and down in the air.

"Lex, look how far I can leap in the air," I *mented*.

Lex watched and she tried it too.

I began to make cartwheels and somersaults and round-a-bouts all throughout the path. "If only my cheerleading coach could see me now, she would for sure let me be a flyer, instead of a base," I *mented*.

As I was in mid-thought, I suddenly stopped my gymnastics because the most beautiful glowing palace stood before me. It was shimmering a royal blue, the same color as the Vigor Juice.

The palace was majestic, and it looked like it was floating in the pink sky. It extended endlessly, and had beautiful wraparound balconies trimmed in gold. I couldn't have imagined a more fitting palace if I tried.

"Welcome, star seeds, we have arrived at the Alcazar," Artie *mented*.

"Why do you keep calling us star seeds?" Lex asked inquisitively.

"Aha, you've caught on," Artie *mented*.

"Well, what does it mean?" Lex asked.

"There is no better time to ask this question than now. Your senses are getting stronger and you are beginning to feel things intuitively. Come with me and you shall see," Artie *mented*.

As Artie bounced around we followed him. He stopped, looked at us, and said, "The Alcazar is our headquarters. We activate star seeds here, among other things."

CHAPTER 20

ALEXA

Whoa. This place was immense. I needed to get up and explore. Feeling like a princess, I twirled around on the translucent floors.

The entrance of the palace was ornate, with marble and gold columns everywhere. A grandiose circular staircase was in the middle, and the hallway went on as far as I could see.

"Look at my feet, they're activating shades of purple! Plum, orchid, and grape," I *mented*. Artie and Jay watched me twirl around the floor.

"Come along, on your purple path of enlightenment," Artie *mented*.

I continued twirling. I was a little dizzy but I saw all the shades of purple forming below me. I couldn't stop. I spun on and on, round and round. "Oops ... oh sorry, excuse me," I *mented*.

A dazzling Arcturian put her hands out and batted her long lashes in the air. She was coming to embrace me with a tremendous hug. She had golden curls that flowed down her small Arcturian frame and large, green almond-shaped eyes. She stood about the same height as Artie. Her gold robe trailed behind her down the corridor.

She looked at me and Jay excitedly and *mented*, "Alexa, Jaycee! I am so excited to finally meet you. Oh give me a big hug quickly before I burst out my Vigor."

"Hi, um ... who are you? You're so pretty," I said shyly.

She liked this and smiled. "I'm Sofia. Guardian of the Dipper, princess of the dynamic Arc, mother of all Creations, and lover of life."

Artie looked at Sofia and chuckled, "A simple princess would do, sweetling," Artie *mented*.

Sofia spun around and around, letting a beautiful rainbow of colors spill out around her.

Artie whispered in my ear, "She can be a little dramatic."

Sofia stopped abruptly and dashed over to Artie. "I heard that, Artie. Girls, don't listen to him. Artie is just a little sore that I had to step in and help the Wiley brothers with that leftover karma. Bullying will get you nowhere, girls. Artie was fumbling around trying to round up you little ladies back on Earth, and of course, it was Sofia to the rescue. Don't worry, Marty Artie, I took care of it," Sofia *mented* with a wink.

"I call him Marty too!" Jay said loudly.

Sofia gave her a knowing glance. "Oh don't I know it, Jay. You are quite the feisty one, I see." Sofia led us into a bounce, leaving Artie slightly behind.

"Hey, those are my star seeds, wait up," Artie *mented* and quickly bounced to catch up.

I really liked Sofia. She was so much fun. I wondered what all that talk was about, though.

I felt something was on my wrist. I looked down and I couldn't believe what I saw. It was Indigo! How did she get there?

"Jay, look over here, Indigo is back and on my wrist," I *mented*.

"She found us," Jay *mented*.

Artie and Sofia were smiling. I put my arm out, and Indigo fluttered around me.

"Come along now, girls, we don't have much time, Indigo will come with us," Sofia assured.

We continued to bounce around the long hallway corridor arm in arm.

"Where are we going, Sofia?" I *mented*.

Sofia looked at me and said, "To the EverCore, of course."

CHAPTER 21

JAYCEE

I watched my footsteps create rays of purple but they weren't as vibrant as Lex's path.

"Step into my office, let's have a chat," Artie said. Once again, a couch appeared behind us.

"Artie, you have to teach me how to do that," I *mented.*

"Jay, remember in the cave when I told you that I knew about what happened with the girls at camp. Are you okay?" Artie asked.

I looked down in embarrassment and felt a knot in my stomach. Why had he brought that up again? I'd never felt so badly about my friends.

"Not really Artie, I'm sad and mad too ... mad that I let them say those hurtful things to me," I responded.

Artie put his little arm around me. "I thought so. I can see it in your energy. What Tiff, Jen, and the rest of the girls did was truly wrong and hurtful. There is no doubt about that. Do you know what you can do that will be best for you?" Artie asked.

"What should I do?" I questioned.

Artie looked at me with his kind oversize green eyes. I felt his love and concern in an unspeakable way.

"Forgive," Artie said encouragingly.

"Forgive, no way, Artie. They hurt me, I can never be friends with them again," I blurted out.

"You will, you'll see." Artie *mented.* "We all make mistakes. Your energy levels are declining because you are harboring negative thoughts and feelings. When you are able to forgive, you will raise your vibration and fully utilize your power-points. That will give you your powers," Artie assured me.

My powers? I have powers? And power-points? My eyes brightened up. What exactly could that mean?

"That's why we are at the EverCore. Come with me and you shall see."

We stood at the carved doors, and Indigo flew to Artie to perch on his shoulder. Pitter patter, pat, pat, Artie was doing some sort of detailed knock at the door. The door opened, almost magically, but I was beginning to learn that here, out by Arcturus, it wasn't magic at all.

Lex and I skipped into an open room filled with bright light. The room was surrounded with floor-to-ceiling windows that looked out at the pink sky, high-peaked purple mountains, and royal blue fountains. I gazed out at the view and searched the cloud-covered grounds for my koala-like friend. I wondered where he was hiding.

I scanned the grounds below and saw a blue furry speck sitting below a purple palm tree. Of course, I thought: Izzy's a creature of comfort. I giggled to myself.

I returned my gaze to the room. Rays of colors beamed in the air. Hundreds of Arcturians stood around the room, each at his or her own translucent desk.

"What are these desks?" I *mented.*

"These are not desks, these are our Dippers," Artie *mented.* "Welcome to the EverCore, girls. This room is the epicenter of our headquarters, this is where all our work is done."

"Work? What kind of work?" I *mented.*

Sofia chimed in, "This is where we send our love and energy back down to Earth."

Each Arcturian was illuminating a specific color from his or her Dipper. With all the Dippers at work, the room was forming huge rainbows. There were seven desks for each row.

"Do you know why there are seven per row, seedlings?" Artie asked.

Before Lex and I could come up with the answer, Sofia interjected, "Seven power-points, seven desks, seven colors, but of course."

"Ms. Know-it-all Sofia, I was asking our star seeds," Artie *mented.*

Lex and I cracked a smile of relief. I looked around the room at all the Dippers. The rows went way back, I couldn't even see where they ended. Each Dipper in every row radiated a specific color: the first was red, the second was orange, the third was yellow, the fourth was green, the fifth was blue, the sixth was violet, and the last was dark purple.

"What does each color mean, Artie?" I *mented.*

"Good question, Jay. Each power-point is connected to a specific color and has a different function and purpose. The Arcturians in this room work on helping their designated star seed develop his or her power-point on Earth."

"It's a lot like what we are doing here with you, but you girls get the red carpet tour," Sofia *mented.* She gazed at our amethysts and winked.

"The purple power-point!" Lex gasped.

"Wait, hold on, how are you able to work with people on Earth? How is that possible when you are here at Arcturus, so far away?" I *mented.*

"We use these Dippers to send vibrations to our star seeds on Earth."

"But how do you send vibrations through a desk? Sorry, I mean Dipper," I corrected myself.

"We DIP," Artie explained.

"DIP?" I repeated and scrunched up my face, confused.

"Yeah, DIP, which means we go Down the Insight Pathway, to Earth," Artie responded.

Artie walked over to the middle of the room and motioned for us to join him.

There was a silky golden cloth covering something. Artie carefully removed the cloth to unveil a ginormous, translucent Dipper. It was at least four times the size of the ones that we'd seen. It was the same size as Artie.

"This is the Mega Dipper," Artie stated.

"Are you showing off, Artie?" I chuckled.

"Of course he is," Sofia said, with a wink.

"When we DIP, we are sending messages through the galaxy. The energy travels far but fast, and it will be delivered into a star seed's head in the form of messages," Artie said.

"What? I am confused," I admitted.

"Let us show you," Sofia insisted.

"The mission list, please," Artie requested.

A clipboard appeared in his hands. I was getting used to these type of happenings, I thought.

"Aha, mission Ashley under way, off to Denver, Colorado we go," Artie *mented.*

Sofia read the briefing over Artie's shoulder. She nodded her head periodically as he continued.

"Ashley loves to cook, like you Lex, but lately she is sad because her best friend moved away to a different state. Ashley has been sulking in her bedroom instead of doing the things she enjoys. Cooking is something she is passionate about. It brings her love and happiness. When she is doing something good for herself and igniting her own self-love, she is actually giving the universe back love when she cooks," Artie informed.

"Let's help Ashley out of her sadness," Sofia encouraged.

"Well, how are *we* going to do that?" Lex asked, rubbing her cheeks.

"We're going to DIP!" Sofia *mented.*

"This is so hard for me to comprehend," Jay whispered in my ear.

Sofia heard me. "No, Jay, it's really quite simple. Think of the Dipper as a big window into Earth, like a telescope. We can travel anywhere, to any location, any house, building, structure, and DIP into any room," she explained.

"Is this how you know things about us?" I *mented.*

"It's one of the ways," Artie *mented.* "Watch, and do as I do."

ALEXA

Artie closed his eyes and touched the Mega Dipper, which began to emit bright green rays of light. "Tune into my thoughts."

I did as Artie suggested.

Something orange, green, and red,
C'mon, Ashley, get out of bed.
Go ahead, cook something yummy.
And good and healthful for your tummy.

The Mega Dipper illuminated green. Artie *mented* the Rhyme Chime one more time, and we watched an image of a girl with brown, shoulder-length straight hair, big blue almond-shaped eyes, and a thin physique rummage around in the kitchen.

Pots and pans clanked together, and carrots, celery, and tomatoes sat on the countertop. Artie and Sofia smiled proudly.

"Carrots, celery, and tomatoes!" I announced, then *mented*, "Orange, green, red." Arcturus was so cool, I never wanted to go back to Earth.

"I'm sorry, my little star seeds, but this is just a training boost; our time with you here is limited," Artie replied to my thoughts.

I really didn't like the thought of leaving such an enchanting place. But it was also weird. I didn't feel sad at all – instead I felt love. How was it possible that the only emotion I had was love? Endless love.

Artie looked at me lovingly and said, "Ah, you're finally getting it, girls, you are figuring us out on your own."

I took a step back from Artie, Sofia, and Jay. Wait a minute, was this really possible? I tried to think of something that would usually make me mad, like when back at school, my classmate, Jason, called me "Lex, the girl with the carrot nose." I couldn't get mad, like I usually would. All I felt was love.

Love so deep and so bright. It radiated and illuminated from my heart to the sky. I saw my feet step and glow deep purple as I twirled around the room. I was so happy. I felt so liberated and full of love on this magnificent star.

There was no Lex, the girl with the carrot nose, up here on this plane. Only happy sentiments and love.

Jay turned to me, "We all hear your thoughts, you know."

I blushed and continued to twirl on.

CHAPTER 22

JAYCEE

I was so glad she stopped caring about her nose as I watched Lex twirl around the room, but I was still just a tad confused. "Does every person on Earth receive messages?" I *mented.*

"Not everyone receives these messages, only the star seeds. It is time to explain how we work."

Artie took our hands as the Arcturians formed a circle around us.

Artie *mented,* and all the Dippers vanished. The room was just a vast, soft cushion. We all spread out comfortably.

"Jay, Lex, we formally welcome you to your Arcturian family," Artie *mented.* "You girls are Arcturian by soul birth."

"Soul birth," Lex *mented.*

"I am not bright pink," I *mented* as I looked down at my arms for reassurance.

"You and Lex have been living among us for hundreds of years," Artie explained.

Suddenly a large, old brown encyclopedia-like book appeared in Artie's hands. It had a big gold lock attached to it. Artie looked at the lock and opened it with his mind.

I stared at the cover. It read, *Our Arcturian Family.* Artie opened up the book with his mind to page 1111.

Page 1111
Jaycee & Alexa Barron, sent to Earth.
Earth parents: Amy & Todd Barron
Reunite with Artie at Camp In-Between

Our eyes lit up. We read the pages intently, and turned them backward to 1093. Artie showed us pages and pages filled with our past lives on Arcturus. But he wouldn't let us read about them.

"I don't want to spoil your quest and purpose. You and Lex now have an idea of what this is all about. We don't want to ruin all the fun," Artie *mented.*

"So let me get this straight: you're saying that Lex and I have been together before? It looks like all these pages are stories about the two of us," I *mented.*

"Yes, Jay, that's right. That is very observant of you. You girls travel together, and you always will."

Lex and I looked at each other as we absorbed this information. I had always felt a strong connection to Lex. I just thought it was a twin thing. I guessed this explained that. I grabbed her hand and squeezed it.

"You girls planned it this way," Artie confirmed and continued, "You know best for one another and always will. Like many other Arcturian star seeds, you have been chosen to manifest on planet Earth as human beings, and to help the Earth receive love. The positive energy you girls share will continue to help the Earth evolve and move into higher dimensions."

"Ah, I get it, you plant us on Earth like a seed," Lex *mented,* beaming.

"Something like that," Artie suggested, and gave Lex a wink. "As our star seeds do their work on Earth, the sky will get bluer, the grass will be greener, the people will be happy and continue to do nice things for one another."

Artie *mented* for all the Dippers to reappear. The Arcturians bounced back to their Dippers, while Lex and I huddled around the Mega Dipper with Artie.

"I have another stop for you girls." Artie swung around and sent out a Rhyme Chime to the universe:

Through the mountains and above the sea,
Take us to the grounds of Camp In-Between.
Out, out and away we go, yippee!

I didn't know if I was ready to see what was going on at camp. I was still tremendously hurt by Tiff and Jen, but

I trusted Artie. There must have been something there he wanted us to see.

The Mega Dipper focused in on the small blue cabin. It was the mess hall. We saw our bunkmates frolicking around and getting their lunch. Tiff was on the burger line twirling her hair, flirting with Danny. Again! I thought.

Phew, Danny didn't engage with Tiff. He turned his head away and talked to the boy in front of him.

"That's Abe," I pointed.

Tiff walked back to the Arcturus table and sat down next to Jen. Tiff banged her hands loudly on the table.

We saw Tiff look at Jen, and then together they glanced at all the girls sitting around the table. Tiff and Jen had all the Arcturus girls' attention. "Girls, are you ready to chant on the count of three," Tiff demanded. "1-2-3...."

But Vee-Vee cut her off, leading a song back at Jen and Tiff. "*You girls are so mean, you think you're all that, but we want Lex and Jaycee back.*"

Celeste interjected and demanded that all the girls stop immediately. "There will be none of that here at this camp. Mrs. Miller will be talking with you very soon," Celeste said sternly.

My heart filled up. I was happy that my bunkmates resisted Tiff's chant. In fact, watching Tiff try to flirt with Danny didn't even bother me.

Strangely, I noticed that I was full of love. There was no anger or sadness in my voice. That must have been forgiveness, like Artie told me. I looked at Lex, and she intuitively knew that I wanted to send Tiff some love.

"Tiff needs a boost to take away her unkind persona," I *mented*.

I looked to Artie and Sofia. They nodded their heads in agreement. I closed my eyes, and *mented* really hard to try and send a Rhyme Chime of my own to Tiff and Jen.

Mean girl, mean girl go away.
Leave our Tiff and Jen today.
Reignite their love and light.
So they shimmer yellow bright.

"Good job, star seed," Artie *mented*. "You're opening your inner strength."

Sofia winked and gazed at my amethyst.

I looked at my necklace, which was beaming brighter around my neck, but I was tired.

"That was hard work. I feel the energy draining out of me," I *mented*.

"Drink some Vigor Juice," Artie said.

Luckily, Lex had already brought me some. I guzzled it down, and my energy returned.

Artie looked at me and smiled. "You are not used to sending out your energy here, so far away from Earth. What you did was wonderful indeed. I am so proud of you that you wanted to do it on your own."

Artie gave us both a big embrace. He covered the Mega Dipper, and we bounced out of the room.

CHAPTER 23

ALEXA

I bounced over to the fountain and drank some Vigor. It was so delicious. The juice tasted like watermelons, just what I had wanted.

I licked my lips after I swallowed the sweet juice. I glanced over at Jay, who'd also been drinking from the fountain. I knew that look. She wasn't talking; that was a sign that she was really tired.

Artie had lots of energy and eagerly *mented,* "Okay, star seeds, there is so much more to see. Let me take you over here, follow me."

Jay stopped in her tracks. "Artie, I can't keep up with all your endless energy. Can we take a nap, please?"

That did sound really nice. "I could use a rest too," I *mented.*

Artie looked at Sofia for her thoughts and pondered Jay's request.

"Have some more Vigor Juice," Sofia insisted.

"I just did," Jay replied. "The DIPping was a lot of work. I need a time-out to gather my thoughts and reinvigorate."

"Hmmm, well, I guess maybe you both need some more time to adjust to our intense energy out here by one of the brightest stars in the galaxy," Artie said.

"We rarely bring star seeds here, so I suppose being fatigued is possible," Sofia said.

Artie pointed his finger up in the air, indicating that he had an idea. "Okay girls, I have the perfect place for you to rest. This way," Artie *mented.*

Artie led us to a room at the end of the hallway. "Sometimes I come in here to listen to my own thoughts. I think this will be a nice place for you girls."

Jay and I entered the room. It was filled with comfy cushions and mats.

"It looks like Think Time," I *mented.*

Artie and Sofia waited at the doorway as Jay and I pulled up two squishy mats next to each other and surrounded ourselves with pillows and blankets before lying down.

"Well don't you two look all cozy in your beds," Sofia *mented.*

"I can't let you girls rest for too long. We don't have that much time left here before I have to get you home," Artie *mented.*

"Oh Artie, let them relax. Don't worry, girls, we'll be back to check on you in a bit," Sofia *mented.*

Artie stood at the door. An Arcturian bounced over and diverted Artie and Sofia's attention. Artie turned back to us and said, "We're needed in the EverCore for a few. We'll be back and when we return nap time is done."

Jay stacked her bed with piles of blankets. She unlatched her amethyst crystal necklace.

"Hey, what are you doing?" I said to Jay.

"I don't think we need these right now. I can't have jewelry on me when I sleep," Jay said.

"It's just a short nap," I said.

"It's cumbersome." Jay set her amethyst down beside her bed.

I looked down at my necklace. I didn't want to take it off. It was so pretty. I turned back toward Jay. I thought she looked a bit translucent. Was it possible that Jay was fading away?

"Jay!" I yelled out loud. "What's happening? Where are you going? Your body is disappearing!" I panicked.

"Lex! Lex! I don't know what's happening," Jay screamed, frantic. "Help me. I feel like I'm getting lighter and out of sorts."

"Jay! You can't go anywhere, especially not without me!" I yelled.

"I don't have any control, Lex, come with me. You can't leave me alone. Please take off your necklace too. Please! Lex, don't leave me."

Oh no! I didn't know what to do. Jay was disappearing. I saw parts of her head and leg but not much more. Then she vanished into thin air. Poof. Jay was gone.

What was I going to do? I couldn't leave her. I had to go find her. I quickly unclipped my necklace, and felt my body traveling, floating, and just like that, I too, was going, going, gone!

CHAPTER 24

JAYCEE

I knew that voice, it was Lex! What a relief that she was with me. I felt around the murky atmosphere for her hand. It was dark. I was able to make out shapes and figures when I squinted my eyes. I looked down at my body and there was nothing there. I touched my leg and I could *feel* it, I just couldn't *see* it. I was invisible. This was really cool but also really *weird.*

"Lex, is that you?!" I screamed.

"Yes, it's me over here, follow my voice," Lex said.

I thought she was next to me. I felt around for her but I still couldn't see anything. Finally, I felt something and grabbed it. Got her!

"Ouch, that's my leg," Lex said.

I moved my hand up, found her arm, and interlocked it with mine. She grabbed my hand for good measure. At least we were together.

"Jay, I can't see you. Can you see me?" Lex asked.

"No, we're invisible, I don't know how we'll get our bodies back."

"Let's try a Rhyme Chime," Lex encouraged.

"We're not in Arcturus," I retorted. "Besides, I already tried. It doesn't work."

"Do you think Artie will get us out of here?" Lex asked.

I hoped so. "How could this have happened?" I questioned. Even though I already knew the answer.

"How will anyone even know where we are?" Lex asked, as she released my hand.

Lex was worried. I knew that she was likely rubbing her cheeks and twirling her hair. I was nervous too. Fear overwhelmed us. In my angst, I let out a high-pitched whistle – something I used to do when I was a child. I had no idea why I chose then to whistle.

"Keep going, it's working," Lex declared.

I whistled some more, and our bodies began to reappear.

"Ha, whistling. Who knew? It's like you cracked some kind of code," Lex said, amused.

I continued to whistle a school cheer repeatedly.

"Jay, stop now," Lex said sharply.

I was taken aback by her sudden bossy tone.

"Jay stop, I mean it. Look around," Lex directed.

I turned my head and realized that my whistling had attracted a swarm of ugly gray figures, and they were headed our way.

These things looked like they had no life in them at all. They were tall skinny figures and had no color, no hue, and no shimmer. But their eyes glowed red.

"Hurry Jay, float faster, we have to get away from these things," Lex said.

"Lex, don't be scared yet. They might be able to help us get back to Arcturus. Let's ask," I said encouragingly.

One of the "things" floated up to us. It was dreary and had a sadness about it. As it came closer I looked at the "thing" with hope, and ignored the desolation in its face.

"Hi," I said. "Can you please help us?"

The thing who we thought was a she just stared at us. Her skin crackled, and her hair was straggly, and she looked frail. The she-thing whistled and spoke in a high-pitched voice.

"Caann Yoouuu Plleeassee Heelpp Uuuss," the she-thing repeated.

I tried again, thinking maybe she didn't understand.

"Can you please help us?" I asked.

"Caaann Yoouuu Plleeassee Heelpp Uuuss."

I rolled my eyes. "Okay, Lex, you try," I said.

"Okaaay Leeex Youuu Trryy."

She really needed to stop doing that.

"Where are we?" Lex asked. Anxiously, I could hear her nibbling on her fingernails.

The she-thing looked at both of us, surprised that we didn't know our whereabouts, and answered, "The Void."

"The Void! The name alone sounds so unwelcoming," Lex quivered.

I was kind of intrigued. "What are you?" I asked. Again the she-thing processed my question.

"Whhhattt aarrree yooooouuu?"

I looked at Lex. This was too weird. Who would have thought that I would have gone from battling mean girls at camp, to trying to communicate with a floating gray thing in a black hole? I was frustrated.

"Listen Miss, we know you understand us. So, maybe you can stop playing games and tell us who you are and how we can get out of here. Are you going to respond to us or just repeat everything we say?" I asked.

She responded in her high-pitched whistle, "My name is Effa. We are The Strays."

As Effa whistled, more Strays appeared in the thick, blacklike haze.

"The Strays? What is that? Why is it so dark here? Where are the pink skies, purple mountains, and blue fountains?" Lex asked.

Effa stared at us blankly. She had no idea what Lex was talking about. Lex panicked.

"Lex, calm down," I said, but she couldn't calm down. Lex let out a big scream. "I want to go back to Arcturus. Artie, Sofia can you hear us?!" Lex shouted.

I closed my eyes and stayed quiet. I tried to *ment.*

"It doesn't work," Lex said sharply.

I let out a sigh and took a long, deep breath.

Lex looked at me with her eyebrows raised and said, "We have to get out of here as fast as we can. I can't believe this, I can't believe you brought us here," Lex sobbed.

I felt so bad. I had to figure out a plan. Effa floated up to my face. I was very uncomfortable as she intruded on my personal space. Effa reached out and touched one of my curls and twirled it around her finger in the air. She held onto my hair. I felt tired.

"Jay, back away," Lex warned me. "We have to get Effa off your hair. She's using it to take away some of your energy."

I looked at Effa and then at my skin as she continued to twirl. Lex was right. I looked at my arm and saw my skin was losing its brightness. I looked at Effa: her skin was changing from gray to a light blue! I tried to pull away from Effa with all my might, but she still clung to my curl.

Lex floated over behind me and said, "I got you, Jay. Lean back on me."

Lex and I latched onto each other.

"When I say go, you tug to release your hair," Lex declared.

We had both of our body strengths to combat Effa.

"Go!" Lex said.

Just like that, I yanked as hard as I could, and I was free.

Ouch, my scalp hurt, I thought as I rubbed it. Despite the ache, I was just glad to be free of Effa's grasp. "I'm tired," I said.

"That's because your energy was being drained," Lex explained.

Effa was upset that she was no longer attached to us and started whistling loudly to the other Strays. In the vast darkness the only thing that we saw were the lights coming from their glowing eyes. With each whistle another Stray appeared, coming at us from all sides. They surrounded us. Panic overwhelmed me. I froze. We were doomed.

CHAPTER 25

ALEXA

"Jay, snap out of it, let's go!" I reached out and shook her arm. "Take bigger strides," I instructed. "We have to hurry. The Strays are gaining on us."

I knew that they were only an arm's reach away. I tried to put on a brave front for the both of us, but I was petrified. Stay calm, Lex, focus, I told myself. I looked at Jay. She was out of her trance and was slowly gliding through the air.

Jay looked over her shoulder. "They are getting really close, we have to get a move on," she said.

I turned my head and got a quick glance. Effa was only inches behind us. Jay moved her arms rapidly. She had a burst of adrenaline. She yanked my arm and was pulling us through the air.

"This must be that fight-or-flight response," Jay said.

"What do they want with us?!" I screamed.

"I don't know, but we don't want to find out," she replied. "Use your arms, to make bigger strides, like you're swimming through the sky."

I spread my arms as wide as I could and swam through the sky. Together, we floated frantically through the dark atmosphere.

I looked behind me to check on the whereabouts of the Strays. I cringed at their proximity. They were manufacturing a slimy glowing substance from their mouths and blowing it into the air.

Slime bubbles were landing all over me. One hit my arm, and I felt liquid ooze out. I kept moving my arms and legs with all my strength, but it felt like I wasn't getting anywhere. I thought I was stuck. I looked over at Jay, and she was immobile too.

I looked around me and saw a thick, opaque web of goo. No wonder we couldn't move.

"Release us! We have special powers, and you wouldn't want us to have to use them on you!" I screamed out to the Strays.

The Strays ignored my demands. The slimy, glowing web thickened. We were trapped.

The Strays hovered around us, and the goo spurted out from their mouths.

"Duck, Lex!" Jay said.

We tried to dodge their bubbles of slime but failed. As they continued to drop on my skin, I could feel my energy was being wiped away. "Artie, please, I beg you, please help get us out of the Void now!" I screamed.

CHAPTER 26

ALEXA

I was overwhelmed with exhaustion. We were attached to the gooey web. I closed my eyes to preserve my energy and pretended that this was all just a figment of my imagination.

"I can't move," Jay mumbled.

"Jay, I'm scared, what are they going to do with us?" I asked nervously.

A Stray twirled my hair and caught me by surprise. I mustered up the strength and opened my eyes. I stared directly at the Stray, and it grabbed me and picked me up out of the web. There was nothing I could do. "Jay, don't let them get me," I said.

"Where are you taking my sister?!" Jay screamed.

Jay was picked up by a Stray and swept out of the web.

"Help us!" we both screamed. We continued to holler, and out of nowhere, a tornado of indigo light came down upon us, spinning around and around above our heads. The swirling tornado sucked us upward and reeled us in.

Jay and I lifted into the funnel of blue, and I felt myself regaining energy and strength. The Strays tried unsuccessfully to pry us from the tornado's firm hold.

"Maybe we are getting out of here," I said in the midst of its grasp.

The force of the funnel broke the slime web apart. The Strays dispersed and were no longer in sight. We were spinning inside the tornado, but its hold was weakening.

"Uh-oh, what's going on? I feel like I am heading back down," Jay said.

"I think I am too!" I screamed, disheartened.

We swirled and spiraled down quickly. The tornado lost its fervor. It disappeared, and we were left floating in the air again.

CHAPTER 27

JAYCEE

"What's happening, Lex? I thought we were going somewhere. Did you realize that the tornado was purplish-blue?" I asked.

"Do you think it was Artie and Sofia?" Lex responded.

"I think so, it was the same color as their shimmer. It had to be them," I said.

"Yeah, maybe they're trying to help us get out of here. What do you think, Jay?"

"I sure hope so," I said.

"Where do you think the Strays went? It's so quiet. Do you think they're hiding somewhere? I am scared, Jay. I don't want them to come back and steal our energy. We have to get out of here, quickly," Lex said.

"Should I whistle?" I asked.

"No way! Why would you suggest that? We saw what happened last time," Lex retorted.

"Well, what do you think we should do, just float around aimlessly?" I said.

Lex started to cry. I did too.

"Jay, I am worried that we'll never get out of here. We didn't even get to see Grandma. Isn't that the whole point of all this, to search for Grandma?" Lex sobbed.

"Yes. Artie was going to take us to her," I said.

"I'm lost and am losing hope fast, Jay. I don't know what's wrong with me," Lex said.

"It's not you Lex, it's being in this dreary, dark place. We can't lose hope just yet. I am determined to lead us out of here. Float with me, Lex. Grab my hand," I advised.

CHAPTER 28

ALEXA

"Grandma, Grandma, please help us," I pleaded.

"There has to be a way out," Jay responded.

Jay squinted her eyes. I followed her gaze and saw something glowing before us. "Jay, is that...?"

"Lex, look! It's Indigo," Jay was excited.

"Indigo!" I gasped. How was she there? She was the only bright spot in the dark atmosphere. Indigo flew over, fluttering her wings, and circled around us. I couldn't believe it.

"Indigo, we are so happy to see you," I called out.

"Can you help us get out of here?" Jay asked.

Our little butterfly stopped her flutter and remained still in the air.

"Oh no, what's happening to her?" I asked.

Indigo shook and stopped. She shook again and stopped. I looked to Jay. "Is she ... what is she doing?"

Indigo shook once more and shot out a butterfly from her own body.

"She's multiplying," Jay said excitedly.

Each butterfly repeated the same motion of shaking and flapping and multiplying into more. There were hundreds, maybe even thousands, of butterflies fluttering around our heads. Walls and walls of colors filled the air.

"Finally there is brightness and color in this ugly place," Jay said.

"How are we going to get out of here?" I said.

We looked at Indigo and all the butterflies around us. They now locked together to form one massive wall. They flew underneath us, and we were lifted into the air.

"We're flying! Lex, this is so amazing," Jay giggled.

"Indigo, where are we going?" I asked.

"Outta here!" Jay declared. "See you later, Void!"

We flew higher and higher, bursting through various atmospheres.

I was so relieved to get out of the Void. I felt safe in the butterflies' protection. Everything looked so much better from up there. The darkness of the Void faded away, and we came to another layer of gloomy sky. We continued to pass it by.

As we traveled the air changed colors: first black, then brown, then yellow and white.

The wall of butterflies gently flattened out beneath us, making a long, wide path. Indigo separated herself from the rest and fluttered up and down.

"Indigo, wants us to walk on this path," Jay declared.

"But it's made of butterflies. I don't want to walk on them. What if we hurt them?" I asked.

"I don't think we will, but there's only one way to find out. C'mon." Jay eagerly stepped onto the path. "This is so cool! This doesn't hurt, right butterflies?" Jay looked down, and the butterflies glowed brighter. This was an encouraging sign.

I had a flashback to when we were leaving camp and Jay was instructing me to climb over the fence. I was scared then too. I hesitated and gently let my feet touch the vibrant path. Jay was right, this was really cool.

We followed it until we reached the last butterfly. We had been led to an immense golden cloud. The cloud was so big that Jay looked like a miniature version of herself.

Jay bent down to touch the cloud. "It's so soft and feels like silk."

I rolled around on the cloud, and Jay joined me. "Mmm, it smells like roses and lilacs," I discerned.

"Look, Lex, there is someone over there waving at us, do you see?" Jay pointed straight ahead, and I looked.

Jay led the way, and we walked toward the figure standing in the distance.

"Her silhouette is large and tall. She shimmers gold," Jay observed.

"It's Grandma," I called out.

CHAPTER 29

ALEXA

"Grandma, Grandma!" I said loudly.

I couldn't believe my eyes. We ran over and gave her the tightest embrace, thrusting all our energy into her.

"Grandma, we knew you would find us. We've been looking for you everywhere," Jay said, out of breath.

Indigo was perched on Grandma's shoulder. I looked at her, our sweet little butterfly. "Thank you, thank you Indigo for bringing us here. Grandma, you have no idea what we have been through. We've missed you more than you could ever know," I said.

"Actually, I do," Grandma responded. "Oh look at my little girls. It's so good to see you," Grandma said.

She kissed us both and gave us a big hug. "My little dumplings, you're not alone. I've been watching you and I always will," Grandma explained.

"Did you see us with the Strays? How horrible that was and without Indigo we wouldn't have gotten back," I said.

Grandma smiled big and bright.

"Grandma, look at you! You are shimmering bright gold," Jay said with excitement. Jay stared at it deeply. "I've never seen anything quite like this color shimmer before. Grandma you've never looked better, so peaceful and elegant," Jay declared.

I looked into Grandma's large turquoise eyes and asked, "If you've been watching us, can you help us get back to Artie and Sofia?"

Grandma's smile turned into a frown. "Oh girls, something terrible has happened."

"What's wrong, Grandma?" I asked.

Grandma grabbed our hands and explained. "I don't know how to best break this news to you so, I'll just tell you. It's Arcturus. Arcturus is under attack."

"Under attack?" Jay and I questioned.

"How could this be? But how and what do you mean?" I asked.

Jay bit her nails nervously. She was quiet and listened to Grandma.

Grandma looked at us both and said, "Well, remember the tornado of energy that came rushing through while you were in the Void?"

We nodded our heads, concerned and curious.

Grandma continued, "The Arcturians sent it with the hopes of zapping you out of there, but it backfired and caused a big blast. There is now a hole in the EverCore. It became a gateway for the Strays to escape the Void."

Oh no! How could this have happened? Jay covered her mouth in shock. I realized what this meant. "So that's why the Strays disappeared. You mean to tell us the Strays are invading?"

"Yes! They are infiltrating it with their draining energy. Girls, you can help save the Arcturians," Grandma advised us.

"We can?" Jay questioned her.

"How Grandma, can you tell us how? We need to save Artie and Sofia and one of the brightest stars in the galaxy," I said.

"Yes, we have to go back. After all, this is all my fault," Jay said.

"It's not your fault, Jay, you didn't know about the necklace," I said.

"Girls listen to me," Grandma instructed. "You have all the powers to do this. We will have to get you girls back there, and you need to get those necklaces. They are the key to opening up your inner strength."

"Inner strength? We could barely fight off those Strays in the Void," I said.

"How are we supposed to do it *there*?" Jay asked.

We huddled close together as Grandma gave us celestial advice. "Girls, you'll know what to do once you have the necklaces back. Just *ment* to me once you have them, and I'll help you from there," Grandma assured us.

"Grandma, are you able to come with us?" I asked hopefully.

"I'm always with you. I'm watching you wherever you are. Now go, there isn't much time," Grandma replied and kissed our foreheads.

The butterflies formed another big, bright, beautiful path, and Indigo assumed her position and led the way.

Grandma looked at Indigo and then back at us. "My dumplings, you must go," she said. "They need your help and every second counts."

I ran over and gave Grandma one last bear hug, and so did Jay. Together, we followed the butterfly path because we had to get back to Arcturus fast.

CHAPTER 30

JAYCEE

Why did I have to take off that necklace?! I was determined to fix the mess. All I could think about was how were we going to save one of the brightest stars in the galaxy? What kind of powers did we have? I knew that we needed a plan. I thought back to our necklaces.

"Lex! How are we even going to be able to reenter the atmosphere if we don't have our amethysts?" I asked.

"I don't know, we'll just have to wait and see," Lex told me.

"I guess if the Strays can get in, so can we," I said.

I looked at the butterflies weaving us through the air. Nobody would ever believe this. We floated through the atmosphere on our carpet of butterflies. As we flew, I could see a familiar big orange star in the near distance. It seemed less bright, though – a bit faint and dull.

"Arcturus! We're back on the Arcturian plane," Lex said.

I looked around. Uh-oh. "Look at this place, it's covered in gray!" I said.

Gray sky, gray trees, gray marshmallow houses. It was so sad and dreary. It wasn't anything like the vibrant landscape we remembered.

The butterflies gained momentum and swooped us into the Alcazar.

As we entered the palace, we knew that we had a serious task. We had to find Artie fast.

"Take us to the EverCore, at once," I said to the butterflies. "Artie must be there."

The butterflies picked up the pace, and we used their wing force to blast through the doors of the EverCore.

The Strays were everywhere. In the middle of the room tinkering with the Mega Dipper was a familiar face.

"It's you!" I declared as I stared into Effa's glowing eyes.

"Oh no, we have to stop her fast," Lex *mented*.

Effa looked up at us. "Outta my way, Earthlings. I'll thank you later for giving us our new home," she said to me.

Effa continued to fiddle around with the Mega Dipper. "We have to get this to work," Effa directed to the rest of the Strays.

"My goodness, what a mess, Lex," I *mented*.

"Look, Jay, over there, there is a huge hole in the EverCore," Lex *mented*.

There were pieces of debris everywhere. "Where is everyone?" Lex *mented*.

Lex and I walked over to the big black hole. I felt a strong current as we got closer to it.

"Lex, don't get any closer. It's not just a hole. I think it's an access point into the Void," I cautioned.

I had my eyes on Effa at the Mega Dipper. Effa puckered up her lips. I knew what she was doing. "Lex, quick, duck."

Effa heard me warn Lex and diverted her attention back to me. "Hee-hee-hee. You were lucky once that you got out of the Void, but don't think that you will be spared again," Effa said.

Effa opened up her mouth and blew out a big bubble of goo toward me. The slime flew in the air and I ducked out of the way. I'm too quick for her old tricks. She wasn't going to take my energy again.

"Jay!" Lex hollered. "We need to find Artie, Sofia, and the rest of the Arcturians fast. They must be covered under all this debris. They've got to be in here somewhere," Lex *mented*.

We looked around the room. Luckily, the Strays were preoccupied trying to unlock the Mega Dipper's code.

"Artie," I *mented*.

Artie was on the floor motionless and covered in slime. I knew where *that* came from. This was a sad sight. Artie's eyes looked drained of life, and his body was frail. Sofia was next to him in the same condition.

"We've got to help them," I *mented.*

We picked them up. Their movements were slow, and they were heavy.

Artie opened his eyes sluggishly and *mented,* "Lex, Jay, are you okay?"

Sofia opened up her eyes and wiggled her fingertips. We gave them both a big hug. We could feel how weak they were. They barely had enough energy to embrace us.

"We don't have much time. Arcturus is about to get consumed by the Void. The Strays are getting stronger, ingesting the energy that they've never been able to obtain," Artie told us.

Artie could barely stand up. He closed his eyes again.

"Lex, the Arcturians are fading fast. We have to stop this now. This is all my fault," I *mented.*

"Jay, there's no time to sulk about this. We need to figure out a plan," Lex *mented.*

I got an idea. I looked over at the Strays. They were hovering around the Mega Dipper, practically entranced, while Effa gave instructions from its helm.

"Lex, let's go. I know what to do."

"Are you sure, Jay? Your ideas sometimes don't pan out too well..." Lex *mented,* hesitating.

"Just trust me," I *mented.*

We told Artie that we would be right back. Meanwhile, it looked like Effa had cracked the code to unlock the Mega Dipper.

"Aha! I think I figured it out!" Effa screamed. "Strays, prepare to slime." She looked through the flat screen of the Mega Dipper.

The Arcturians watched in horror as Effa got closer to accessing the Mega Dipper. The Arcturians were too weak to get up from the floor to stop her.

I ran out the EverCore's doors. We didn't have much time. "Lex, hurry up!" I called.

"Jay, where are we going?" Lex asked behind me.

We ran down the hall. "Faster. Just follow me." I flung open the door to the Meditation Room. "The necklaces.

We've got to find them," I urged. I frantically searched for them.

"Are we in the right room?" Lex asked.

"Yes, this is it," I told her. "Do you remember where we put them? I thought they were next to our beds."

"I don't see them, Jay," Lex informed.

"Look harder, they have to be here," I directed.

Lex pulled the covers and pillows off her bed and shook them out, but there was nothing there. I saw a small cubbyhole and noticed something shimmering. I walked over.

"I found them!" I said joyfully. "Lex, clip mine on and I'll do yours."

We looked at our amethysts now fastened securely around our necks. "Let's go, Lex!" I *mented.*

I grabbed Lex's arm, and we ran out of the room back toward the EverCore.

Inside we saw hundreds of Strays filling the room, all focused on Effa. A group of them, following her signals, made small adjustments to the Mega Dipper and looked to her for further directions. I pushed my way to the Mega Dipper and approached Effa at its controls.

"Effa!" I called out. "We have something to share with you." We stood in front of her.

"What is it, my soon to be fellow Strays?" Effa asked.

Lex and I stared into Effa's glowing eyes. "Stand back, Arcturians," Lex and I *mented,* "and let us do our work."

We leaned against the Mega Dipper with our backs touching the flat screen. Effa stood in front of us. The Strays seemed frozen, as if stuck "on pause" without her guidance.

"Nothing you girls have to say or do will change yours and this star's fate," Effa proclaimed.

"Okay Lex, *ment* as hard as you can to Grandma," I said, determined.

Lex nodded her head. I rubbed my amethyst crystal necklace as I *mented,* "Grandma we're ready for you. Help us open up our inner strength."

We did exactly what Grandma told us. My amethyst started to glow as I rubbed it.

"Lex, quick, rub your amethyst." I *mented*. Lex started to rub hers as we continued to *ment* to Grandma. "Jay, nothing is happening. Where is Grandma?" Lex *mented*.

Effa looked at us, laughing and pointing. "Nice try, you silly Earth girls. Now stand back. Strays, get ready to slime."

"Try harder, Lex!" We closed our eyes and *mented* harder.

Our amethysts glowed but nothing happened. "My head is starting to hurt," Lex *mented,* and she rubbed the center of her forehead.

An indigo glow shone from that very spot on her brow as she continued to rub it.

"Lex! Keep doing that," I *mented,* and I did the same.

"Open up your inner strength," Grandma's voice repeated in my head.

We rubbed our amethysts and simultaneously rubbed our foreheads. We said the Rhyme Chime that Grandma gave us three times:

Strays, you bring Arcturus strife
And suck the spirit from our life.
Restore love to this special place –
Back to the Void your dreary face.

Warm gusts of air funneled around the whole star. The gust made its way into the pores of the Arcturians' skin and began restoring their shimmer back to a bright blue.

"I feel the energy coming back," Artie declared.

"Look, the Strays are fading away," I *mented.*

The Strays were disappearing in the very same way that Jay and I got zapped into the Void.

"Hooray!" Lex cheered.

The Strays continued to vanish from the warm, loving air.

"No, you can't do this to us, stop this at once!" Effa screamed, frightened.

"Go back to the Void, Strays," I said.

Effa faded fast. Her body disappeared first, and only her head was visible. "She looks kind of funny with just a head," I laughed.

"No, you can't do this to us!" Effa shrieked. Suddenly, Effa was totally gone.

"What goes around, comes around," Lex said.

I gave Lex a high five. We celebrated as the enormous hole in the EverCore closed up and all the Strays returned to their desolate place.

CHAPTER 31

JAYCEE

Artie and Sofia beamed. Together, we watched joyfully as the magnificent star came back to life. A curtain of butterflies encircled the room.

The Creations came out of hiding. The trees and mountains were purple, the sky was a pearly pink, the fountains returned to a royal blue. The ground was bouncier than ever before. Arcturian harmony and love were fully restored.

Artie looked at us with a tear running down his face. "This is not a sad tear, it's a happy one. You did it, star seeds! You saved us. Your powers together are tremendous. How did you know how to use your necklaces like that?" Artie *mented.*

I giggled playfully and admitted, "We had a little help along the way." I winked at Lex.

Lex winked back, "We found Grandma, Artie. She helped get us out of the Void."

"Ah, I see," Artie replied, as Indigo flew to his side.

"Actually, it's all thanks to Indigo. She led us to Grandma," I said.

"Grandma told us Arcturus was under attack and she gave us the Rhyme Chime," Lex added.

Artie's eyes beamed with pride.

"We are so proud of our star seeds. You saved us and our star," Sofia said.

"We just fixed what we did. Well, what I did," I said sadly. "If I hadn't taken off my crystal necklace, you all would never have been in this mess," I admitted.

"Nonsense! This was a test, to see if you girls could connect to your inner strength. You persevered and have taken our home to brighter heights," Artie declared. "Your loving powers and intentions have multiplied, and you will take these back with you to Earth. You girls have come into your powers magnificently."

Lex and I looked at each other and simultaneously said, "A test?"

"Yes, life is a series of tests to help us grow." Artie continued. "With every challenge successfully completed, we strengthen our own powers. You have awakened your purple power-point, and it has opened up immensely. You are strong, independent, filled with self-love and inner strength."

"You can see that in us?" I asked.

"Absolutely," Artie proclaimed.

ALEXA

I gulped down some Vigor. Pineapple and mango, yum. Jay gulped some down too.

"Mmm, chocolate milkshake," Jay grinned.

"Girls, it's time, we have to get going and return to Earth," Artie *mented.*

"No wait, before we go, can we DIP in and see what's going on?" Jay asked.

I thought Jay was still affected by Tiff and Jen's behavior. She probably wanted to see what happened after she DIPped the Rhyme Chime to Tiff and Jen.

"Okay, let's go, DIP in quickly," Artie said.

Jay led us over to the Mega Dipper, where she repeated the original Rhyme Chime:

Through the mountains and above the sea,
Take us to the grounds of Camp In-Between.
Out, out and away we go, yippee!

We watched as the Mega Dipper focused in on camp. We saw Mrs. Miller, Celeste, and the camp leadership team rushing around the campgrounds calling out our names.

"Alexa, Jaycee!" Mrs. Miller bellowed.

Celeste combed the woods behind the bunk with other counselors in tow. "Lex, Jay, where are you?" she called.

"I feel bad. Everyone is looking for us. We have to get back to camp," I urged.

Jay remained silent and watched intently. I could tell that she was still unsure. The Mega Dipper refocused and showed us a new image. We viewed a different location, a pond, with coins being thrown into it rapidly.

"The wishing well," Jay *mented.* The Mega Dipper readjusted. "Look," Jay pointed. It was Tiff, Jen, Vee-Vee, and all the other girls in our bunk. They were frantically throwing coins in the pond.

A thought, a hope, a wish, a dream.
I ask for help, my fish agleam:
This coin holds my intentions.
Take them through vast dimensions.
Return them here—Camp In-Between.

"I hope this will help bring Lex and Jay back," Tiff said.

"Keep wishing," Jen said.

"I feel so bad. We were so mean. Jay didn't deserve that," Jen said.

"Jay is my best friend, I would do anything to have her back," Tiff said.

"Keep wishing," Jen suggested.

The Mega Dipper zoomed back out, and the image fizzled away. I was surprised and relieved that our bunkmates were wishing for us to come back.

"Lex is right. We should return to camp. It's time," Jay declared.

"I want to soak up everything here. I wish I could take this place with us," I *mented* and continued to gulp down Vigor and bounce around the room. The purple shades emanating from my feet were bigger and brighter than before. I twirled around the room. I felt safe, happy, and filled with love.

"Arcturus is a part of your DNA, and it will never leave. You're going to make several trips back here to work on your other power-points. This is just the beginning of your galactic journey," Artie advised us.

"Really?!" I said excitedly.

"You and Jay will be able to visit us many times again. You'll see. This is just a farewell for now, not a good-bye," Artie *mented*.

"You have a job to do back on Earth. We are just helping you learn how to use your innate tools," Sofia *mented*.

"Remember, girls, you are gifted with your inner strength. When you apply it, you are sending out rays of love to the Earth," Artie *mented*.

Jay and I listened intently.

"Group hug," Jay *mented*.

"Good-bye, Arcturus, we'll be back soon," Jay waved her hands in the air.

"I hate good-byes. I mean farewells," I sobbed out loud.

"Don't worry, Lex, we'll be back," Jay said and hugged me tight.

CHAPTER 32

ALEXA

We followed Artie out of the EverCore and through the Alcazar's doors. We strode the same white walkway that had brought us here. Artie led us over to a blue fountain and brought us behind it, unlocking a secret door.

"A secret hideaway," I *mented.* At this point I expected nothing less.

Artie flashed me a quick wink and pulled out two paper scrolls, each tied with a golden bow. "I've been keeping these safe for you girls," Artie *mented.* He handed one to Jay and one to me.

"These are your star maps. It's your life guide," Artie instructed.

Jay and I looked at each other.

"A map to our life?" we *mented.*

"Can we see our future?" I asked.

Jay was just as confused as I. Artie opened up one of the maps. It was filled with lines that connected to numbers and dots. It looked like a puzzle of some sort.

"These maps will be instrumental in the future. Think of them as a code that you have to unlock. You will not use them yet. Just watch out for the signs, and you'll know when you need them," Artie *mented.*

"This looks way too complicated," Jay said.

"I agree, I don't know how we'll ever understand these maps," I said.

"Girls, I don't want to confuse you, but these are very important and a huge part of the reason why I brought you here. We are all guided by the stars in the sky, whether we understand it or not. Your life, my life, your parents' lives, we all have our own special map and are free to use it and learn about it. Not everyone gets them handed out like I'm doing with you girls. So consider yourselves very lucky. Just be open to receiving the signs and messages. Easy as pie," Artie *mented.*

"No wonder I have always been so intrigued by the stars," I *mented.* It was all starting to make sense. "Thanks, Artie. I can't wait to learn all about my star map."

Jay looked at her scroll, still perplexed. "Well, I guess I'm going to try really hard not to lose this," Jay *mented.*

I took the scroll from Jay's hands. "I'll keep it safe for us."

"Okay girls, let's move on, shall we?" Artie closed the secret door and continued to bounce with us down the buoyant path.

CHAPTER 33

ALEXA

Whoosh, the portal sucked us in. Like an elevator we were going up, up, and away, and then side to side. Thump. It stopped.

"Alright, my star seeds, we are here. Come walk this way, on the golden cloud," Artie instructed.

"Hey, we know this place," Jay called out.

"Grandma! This is the best surprise ever," I said as I rolled around in the cushiony clouds.

Jay did a big cartwheel. I was so excited. We both somersaulted around in the rose- and lilac-scented clouds.

"Over this way," Artie directed, and we tumbled to the left. Grandma shone so radiantly, but she was not alone. A large group of people were gathered around her, people we didn't know.

Behind Grandma there was a large mahogany table with ten tall, gold velvet chairs. We watched as everyone took a seat.

Grandma put her index finger against her mouth, gesturing for us to keep quiet. We observed in silence and looked around the table, not believing our eyes.

Jay, Grandma, and I took up three of the seats. "How can this be? We are right here, how are we also there?" I asked Jay in disbelief. "It's like watching ourselves in a movie."

Seated in the fourth chair was a boy who looked so familiar to me. I thought and thought and thought, who can this be? Then Jay let out a big gasp and whispered, "Lex, that's Danny!"

JAYCEE

My heart sunk a little seeing him. I had forgotten how much I liked Danny. The last time I saw him we were covered in paint and I ran away from him. I felt so bad. I bet he didn't like me anymore. Why was he there with Grandma? It was so strange. I watched as Danny received a paper being passed around the table. He took a pen and signed his name.

"Who are the rest of the people sitting in the chairs?" I asked.

"We don't know them," Lex replied.

Grandma looked at us both and whispered, "Not yet."

Everyone at the table was reading from a few sheets of paper. It appeared that they were all reading the same thing. They nodded periodically and signed their names, as they passed the paper around the table.

Finally the paper reached Lex and me (well, the Lex and me sitting at the table). It *was* like watching myself in a movie. We were the last ones to sign the paper.

I exhaled and said, "Grandma, we just signed our name on that paper, too."

"Of course you did, Jay. That is your soul contract," Grandma said.

Artie smiled and said, "That's why you are here. This is what you need to see. The people who enter your life are not coincidences at all. You chose them back in time."

"We did?" I asked, surprised.

Lex's mouth hung open wide in amazement and disbelief.

"What about Danny? Why is he here? You mean, we chose each other too?" I asked.

"Yes, that's right, Jay. You and Danny have a special connection, but that's all I can say. You'll have to find out for yourself along the way," Grandma said with a smile.

"I knew it. We have the same skin shimmer, so I knew something was up. I can't wait to tell him," I said excitedly.

"You probably won't remember this when you get back to Earth. Don't worry, we will send you signs and rhymes," Grandma reassured us.

"Why won't we remember this, Grandma?" I inquired.

"It will preclude you from growing, my little dumplings; but one thing I can assure you girls is that you travel together. You have and you always will," Grandma said.

Travel together, I thought. What does that mean?

"Lex and Jay, you are deeply linked, not just as twin sisters. Your energies are part of one another for eternity. You are Forever SoulSisters," Grandma admitted to us.

"Wow," I said. I looked at Lex, and a gigantic smile as big as the sky flowed across my face. Lex and I embraced in a warm, delightful hug and put our pinkies out.

Our pinkies interlocked, and we said cheerfully, "Forever SoulSisters, that's us."

Our pinkies lingered together for a little longer.

"Now, my little dumplings, go on, you've got work to do," Grandma directed. "I will send you my love and have Indigo follow you." She kissed and hugged us farewell.

"Watch for me in your dreams, and when you see your Mom and Dad back on Earth, give them a hug and you'll feel me with you," Grandma said.

Our eyes filled with tears. "We love you, Grandma," Lex and I called out as we parted ways.

Artie led the way back, and we started rolling along the same path that smelled like roses and lilacs.

"Here we are, back at the golden cloud," Artie said.

"Artie, are you coming with us?" I asked.

"Yes, my star seeds, I will travel along to make sure you get back to Earth safely. Once we get there, I will have to let you go off on your own."

CHAPTER 34

ALEXA

"Girls, it's safe, we're back, open your eyes," Artie said joyfully. We were back in the cave where we first met Artie. The cave was filled with animals, plants of all kinds, and Indigo fluttered right beside us. I was really happy to be back.

"Harold, you're here!" I was thrilled to see my friend and couldn't wait to tell him everything about our trip.

"What took you so long? I don't know a thing about time or space, but it feels like forever. I'm so glad you're back," Harold told me.

"Harold! We have so much to tell you. I'm sorry you couldn't come with us," I said.

"Yeah, no worries, I like staying here. I've kept all the animals company here in this cave," he joked.

"Maybe next time you'll venture off Earth with us," I said jokingly.

Harold shrugged. Jay and Artie stood off to the side.

"Harold missed us," I said.

"Well, now that we are all reunited, let's get going. Perhaps Harold can lead the way back to camp," Artie suggested.

"Harold says he would be happy to," I translated to Artie and Jay. All together we skipped up and down the windy mountain terrain holding hands.

I was sad that Artie was leaving us. I had become attached to our galactic guide. I looked into Artie's large almond-shaped eyes.

Artie looked at me and saw the tears falling on my cheeks. "Oh don't be sad, my little star seed. Our voyages have only just begun. You will be seeing a lot more of me." Artie gently touched my face and wiped away my tears with his hand.

"I'll miss you, little pink man," I said, squeezing his hand.

Jay looked at me and winked. She started humming and singing the cheer that had first brought us there, so appropriately. Jay sang, and we followed her lead.

Red as the roses that sprout from the ground.
Yellow, so yellow, the sun it shines down.
Orange is sweetness that grows on the trees.
Green is for goodness, the earth and the leaves.
Blue is the sky, and it's deep as the sea.
Purple, so vibrant and pure as can be.
The rainbow of colors surrounds you and me.

We cheered and skipped through the mountains and headed down into the valley. We arrived at the outskirts of the camp, where the wooden gate that I had trouble going over was fortunately propped open.

"They must have forgotten to lock it when they went looking for us," Jay said.

Artie turned to us with his warm eyes. "Okay, girls, my journey ends here. I don't want anyone to see me," Artie said.

"Artie, when will we see you again?" Jay asked, concerned.

Artie put his arm around us and squeezed us tightly. "Don't worry, girls, I'll always DIP in," he winked. "Don't forget about the powers in your necklace. Whenever you feel unsure, rub it and think about your intention." Artie touched our necklaces and filled them with extra-special love. They beamed so brightly around our necks.

We said our farewells to Artie. I felt his unconditional love, and just like magic, Artie disappeared.

CHAPTER 35

JAYCEE

Lex and I grabbed hands and walked through the open gate into the grounds of Camp In-Between. I couldn't help it, I was nervous to face those girls again.

Clank. The gate closed behind us. We saw bunk Arcturus a few feet away.

"Do you think they're here?" I asked.

"I don't know," Lex said and shrugged her shoulders.

We walked into the bunk. It was empty. We dropped our backpacks on our beds. My bed was covered with cards of all sorts. Handmade cards, painted, glittered, and filled with stickers. I held the cards in my hands and went through the pile. Thirteen in total.

Twelve of them were from all the girls in the Arcturus bunk, and each one said, "I'm Sorry, Please Forgive Me." There were even cards from Tiff and Jen.

I picked up another note that was different from all the rest. It was a letter on loose-leaf paper. "Jay, where are you? From Danny."

He missed me, I beamed. I really thought that after the dance party, he wouldn't like me for running out like that. I didn't think we would ever talk again. I showed Lex the cards as we put them on the side of my bed. I was relieved.

"That was really nice of the girls. Let's go find them and let them know we're back," Lex said.

Lex opened the bunk's front door and I followed her.

We walked up and down the rolling hills of the camp. "Look, Jay, over there at the boat lake, I think that's Celeste and the rest of our bunk," Lex said.

Before we knew it, Mrs. Miller was walking toward us blowing a whistle and waving her hands in the air. "Lex, Jay, where have you been? Oh thank goodness you are back. You've had us so worried. We've been looking all over for both of you."

Mrs. Miller wrapped her arms around us and gave us a big squeeze. "I must call your parents and let them know that you girls have safely returned," Mrs. Miller said anxiously.

Mrs. Miller pulled out her cell phone from the back pocket of her denim shorts. She couldn't wait to share the good news. We heard our Mom through the phone say hello.

Mrs. Miller said, "Hi, Mrs. Barron, this is Rhonda over at the camp. We have some excellent news. Jay and Lex are here safe and sound. I'm so sorry for the worry." Mrs. Miller listened to Mom talk and then said, "You don't have to come to camp, all is fine." She listened again and said, "Ah yes, of course, I completely understand. So when can we expect you at camp?"

Lex and I looked at each other. Our parents were on their way to camp?

Mrs. Miller said good-bye and hung up the phone. She turned to us. "Your parents are so happy that you are safe. They want to take you with them for a few days. You know, just so you girls have a proper chance to say your good-byes to your Grandma."

Mrs. Miller put her phone back in her shorts' pocket and placed her arms around us. "I am just so glad you girls are back. What a scare! What a scare!"

"Come with me, I'll take you to join the rest of the girls in your bunk," Mrs. Miller said. "Everybody will be so happy to see you. What a relief."

Mrs. Miller looked at Jay and said, "I want you to know, we are taking the incident very seriously and following our protocols. We already spoke to the girls in your bunk, and they are aware that their behavior was wrong and hurtful."

"Thanks Mrs. Miller. I really do appreciate your concern," I said gratefully.

I was relieved that Mrs. Miller spoke with the girls in our bunk. Lex was right, telling her was the right thing to do. I felt so lucky that Lex always looked out for me.

CHAPTER 36

ALEXA

Mrs. Miller escorted us over to the boat lake. I wondered how Jay was feeling about the other girls. I looked over her way. "Jay?" I said.

Jay was distracted, and something was moving around in her pocket. What was that? Yup, that was definitely a little head sticking out of her sweatshirt. How did she keep whatever was there a secret from me?

"Mrs. Miller, we'll catch up to you. I have to talk to Lex for a minute," Jay said, as she pushed the creature back down into her pocket.

"Okay, but hurry up, girls. I'm keeping my eyes on both of you," Mrs. Miller instructed.

"Jay, what's going on in there? Is there something moving around in your pocket?" I asked.

"Shh," Jay said, as she pulled out a Buskey.

"Oh wow, Jay! Did you take him from the Creation Station?"

Jay smiled and laughed. "No! I swear I have no idea how he got in here." Jay's necklace started to glow brighter around her neck.

"Artie!" I said.

"It must have been a gift," Jay suggested.

"I am so glad he reconsidered. I guess Creations don't have to stay back at Arcturus after all," I giggled, and so did Jay.

I took the Buskey from Jay and petted him. He was so cute, and I was glad we had a part of Arcturus with us.

Just then Mrs. Miller turned her head toward us. I was worried that she was going to see the Buskey. She looked at us and said, "Girls, come along, everyone's waiting for you."

I held the Buskey as Mrs. Miller walked over to us. I cringed. I was nervous that she wasn't going to let us keep him.

Somehow, she couldn't see him! He was invisible to her. I was relieved. "Okay, sorry Mrs. Miller," I said as we resumed walking.

Jay took the Buskey back from me and placed him securely in her pocket.

"What shall we name him?" I asked.

"Hmm, give me a second, I think I know...," Jay said.

"Okay." I waited for Jay.

"How about Nabu?" Jay offered.

I smiled in agreement. "I like that."

"Let's go girls, over to the boat lake," Mrs. Miller said, leading the way.

We saw Celeste's arms waving frantically in the air. She ran as fast as she could over to us and pulled us in for a great big hug.

"We've been so worried about you," Celeste said and rubbed our heads gently.

It felt like she didn't want to let us go. I smiled brightly, and whispered in Celeste's ear, "We went to find Grandma."

Celeste threw her head back, amused. "You did? Did you find her?" she asked gently.

My eyes got bigger and brighter. I knew she would care. "Yes," I nodded my head.

"That's incredible! You'll have to tell me all about it," Celeste said. She gave me another big hug.

Tiff, Jen, and all our bunkmates rushed out of their kayaks, canoes, and paddleboats, and ran toward Jay and me.

JAYCEE

"Our wishes worked!" Jen screamed as she jumped up and down eagerly.

Jen and Tiff approached me with tears running down their faces.

I felt my stomach flutter because I hadn't seen them for so long, and I still felt badly about what they did.

"Jay, listen, we're so sorry that we ganged up against you," Tiff said. "Especially me, you're my best friend and I turned on you."

I felt my heart warm up and the fluttering in my stomach calmed down. Tiff reached for my hand.

"You didn't do anything to deserve that. You were just being you, and I was jealous because I liked Danny too," Tiff admitted. "I am sure that you don't like me, and you have every right to. I don't even deserve a friend like you," Tiff said in front of all our bunkmates, as well as Mrs. Miller and Celeste.

I grabbed Tiff's hand and looked around the bunk. "Tiff, I still like you, but what you and all the girls did was really mean and made me feel really bad. I forgive you, and you're still my best friend. I just hope that you won't do this again."

Tiff looked at me and nodded her head, along with Jen and the rest of the bunk. Tiff touched my purple crystal and stared at it momentarily. "I love your necklace," Tiff said to me. "I've never seen it before. Is it new?"

"Something like that," I said, and winked at Lex.

Celeste moved aside and stepped just out of earshot to talk to Mrs. Miller. When Celeste returned, she said, "Lex and Jay, your parents are in the car on their way to camp. They should be here in a few hours. Would you like to come with us to Pure Treats, where the Canopus boys will be joining us? It's like a cooking-class restaurant."

"Yes," I said with a huge smile on my face.

"I can't wait to cook," Lex said, bobbing her head in the air.

Just as we were about to leave the boat lake for Pure Treats, the Canopus bunk headed our way. I heard a familiar friendly voice calling out my name.

"Jay, Jay, you're back," he said.

It was Danny! I was so excited my heart skipped a beat. My palms got sweaty. I was nervous but ecstatic to see him.

"Danny, Danny," I called out eagerly.

Danny's eyes looked gently at me, and his skin shimmered that familiar turquoise.

"Want to walk to Pure Treats together?" he asked.

"Sure," I said, trying to hold back my excitement.

He put his hand out and took mine in his. We walked together side by side, and I felt a rush of excitement come over me.

Danny looked at me and said, "I have to admit I was worried about you, Jay. I hoped you would come back. I even made a wish at the well."

"You did?" My eyes got wider.

"Shh, no one knows, I snuck away during free swim," Danny said. "Where did you go?"

I paused momentarily. I took a deep breath and said, "Lex and I just needed some space." I smiled inwardly.

"Well, I am just glad you're back. I was hoping that at the next social, you would show me some of your cool dance moves." A big grin spread across his face.

I let out a giggle and nodded my head. A chirping noise came from Nabu. Uh-oh.

"Hey what's that in your pocket?" Danny asked.

I was confused. I didn't think anyone besides Lex and I could hear him. I took my little Creation out and held him in my hand.

"You mean you can see him?" I asked incredulously.

"Yes, of course I can, it's like a baby monkey or something."

Of course he could see it, I thought.

"Danny, meet Nabu," I said proudly, as Danny petted Nabu's head and they became instant friends.

"Jay, I feel like I've known you for much longer than a few days," Danny said.

"Me too. Well, maybe you do," I said playfully and gave Danny a wink.

As we walked to Pure Treats we came to the koi pond. Danny took out a penny from his pocket, looked at me, and said, "Let's make this wish together. Think of a good wish, Jay."

"On the count of three, let's say the rhyme and release the coin," I said. "Ready, One, Two, Three."

A thought, a hope, a wish, a dream.
I ask for help, my fish agleam:
This coin holds my intentions.
Take them through vast dimensions.
Return them here—Camp In-Between.

"Release!" Danny instructed.

We threw the penny in the air and watched it land in the middle of the koi pond.

"What did you wish?" I asked Danny. "I can't tell you or it won't come true," Danny said.

"Yeah, you're right," I agreed.

We stared at each other, and I saw our shimmers connect. They formed a very bright blue light, almost too bright to look at.

Danny squinted from its brightness.

Could he see our shimmer? *Of course* he could, I thought.

"Danny, remember the turquoise paint you got me?" I asked.

"Yeah," he replied. He looked at me as if he was reading my thoughts.

"How did you know that turquoise is my favorite color?" I asked.

He looked intently at our shimmers. "Well, if I told you, you're going to think I'm crazy," he said.

"I don't think anything is crazy anymore," I smiled.

"Come on, let's get going," Celeste called out.

Danny squeezed my hand. Nabu chirped from my pocket.

"Do you think they can see Nabu too?" he asked me, but before I could answer he put his arms around me and kissed me.

"Danny, everyone's watching us," I said.

He looked at me and smiled. "They can't see us if we don't see them. Try it."

I couldn't believe he was using my invisible force field of the antiseeing tactic. He leaned in again and kissed me.

I was so happy in that moment I didn't want it to end. I looked around and took in the majestic scenery. Indigo fluttered around Lex as she led the line of campers and began a familiar cheer: "*Red as the roses that sprout from the ground....*"

CHAPTER 37

ALEXA

We arrived at a small pink house with a black slate roof. The door was open, and out spilled the wonderful fresh scent of apples and honey. French accordion music played from the overhead speakers. We entered a large room, filled wall to wall with murals of colorful fruits and vegetables.

Big copper pots dangled from the ceiling. There were several cooking stations that looked like mini kitchenettes, six to be exact. Out spun a tall, round, and well-groomed jolly chef.

Chef had a big orange beard, small brown eyes, and a smile as large as his face. He was all suited up in his cooking uniform, wearing a white apron and big bulky chef's hat. He danced and sang along to the music, his strides long as he dashed from one end of the room to the other.

"*Bonjour, mes chéries,*" he sang to us. "Welcome to my little heaven. I am Chef Jacques, come in, come in, this is Pure Treats."

I giggled and looked over at Jay. She was laughing with Tiff and Jen. Chef grabbed Vee-Vee's hand and spun her around.

"A little swirl, a little twirl, and we'll do it again," Chef chanted happily.

He spun Vee-Vee one last time before he went over to his desk to turn down the music.

"You've got some moves, Chef," Vee-Vee laughed.

Everyone seemed to have enjoyed the show. I really liked Vee-Vee. I thought she was such a good sport. I secretly wished Chef had chosen me, though.

Chef waddled over to us, spatula in hand. "Come, my little *crème* puffs. Dip in with me to the wonderful world of self-love, and it starts in your tummy." Chef stood there rubbing his tummy at his cooking station. "I hope everyone is hungry because we eat what we cook here. Is everyone hungry?" Chef asked.

"Starved," Vee-Vee replied.

"My little campers, please come closer. We are going to make magic with food," Chef said.

All the campers gathered around the large cooking station in the middle of the room.

"Just so I can get a feel for where to start, raise your hand if you have ever cooked before," Chef Jacques directed inquisitively.

I raised my hand high in the air, proudly. Jay followed slowly behind.

"That's just two." Chef Jacques put his hands to his face, as if he was weeping over this news. "Oh *mon Dieu,*" Chef shook his head back and forth. "Okay, I see we have some work to do."

Chef Jacques took out a variety of fruits and vegetables and placed them on the countertop. "Today we are going to make juices. It's such a hot day that something cool and quenching would be oh so delightful."

"What kind of juices are we going to make, Chef Jacques?" Jen asked curiously.

"I was thinking something simple, like fresh-squeezed limeade," Chef Jacques replied.

I shook my head back and forth disapprovingly.

"What is it? *Ma chérie* with the beautiful green eyes, no good?" Chef Jacques asked, disappointed that I didn't approve.

"I have a juice recipe of my own. It's called Vigor Juice. Would it be okay to share with the class?" I asked.

"Well, sharing is caring, so, of course you can," Chef Jacques said with a smile.

I walked around to the head of the kitchenette with the Chef.

I was so happy to make a tribute to Artie and I hoped he was watching. I wanted him to know how grateful we were to have him around. He showed me how to use my inner strength to overcome some of my fears. I would have never been able to stand in front of the class before our trip to Arcturus.

I distributed a mixture of blackberries, blueberries, beets, and apples to each kitchenette. I demonstrated how to make the Vigor Juice by pressing each fruit and vegetable, one by one, into the juicer. The beautiful red color looked a bit different than our blue Vigor on Arcturus, but it sure smelled amazing. "Okay, time for a little taste," I said to everyone.

"Mmm, yum," Tiff said and licked her lips.

"Lex, this is amazing!" Vee-Vee screamed.

Chef Jacques, meanwhile, had ladled some Vigor into a fancy champagne glass for himself. He closed his eyes and sipped – then smiled and sipped again. "*Bien fait, ma chérie.* Well done!"

I noticed that most of the Canopus boys were watching me. I kind of liked the attention.

I heard Danny say to Jay, "You know most of the boys in my bunk have a huge crush on her. There is a bet on who she will be with."

Jay giggled and smiled. "I guess we'll have to see who she picks," she said.

I blushed, while campers dispersed to the kitchenettes to start making the juice. My heart warmed up, and I noticed how proud I was to be in front of the class and sharing something from Arcturus.

I cleared my throat and announced, "Jay and I want to share this special super-food juice with you. It's an ancient recipe that we've learned from someone very special to us. Legend has it, it's filled with love and will give you a boost of energy, so drink up."

I poured myself a serving and brought one over to Jay. We raised our plastic cups in the air, and I said to Jay, "Here's to Artie."

We clinked our plastic cups together. Jay and I smiled at each other and drank our juices. Everyone left their cups on the Pure Treats counter and lined up by the front door, where Chef Jacques danced while saying his good-byes.

It was already dinner time, and the whole camp was on its way to the mess hall.

"Lex, Jay," Celeste said. "Your parents have just arrived at camp. Mrs. Miller is escorting them to the mess hall."

I was happy Mom and Dad were there, but I was starting to really appreciate camp. We walked toward the mess hall, and then I ran toward Mom and Dad. Jay was embarrassed, her face got as red as a tomato. I knew that she didn't want them to see her with Danny.

Everyone had already gone inside. I heard Jay tell Danny that she would be right back.

Our parents were thrilled to see us. Jay and I looked at each other and we knew what to do. We gave our parents a huge hug.

"I am so happy to see you girls," Mom said.

"Mom and Dad, this hug is from Grandma," I said.

Mom looked at us curiously. I thought she was unsure of how to receive the message. Jay and I looked at each other with big grins. As we hugged our parents, Indigo fluttered around our heads.

"Mom, Dad," Jay said hesitantly.

"What is it, Jay?" our Dad asked.

"Would it be okay if we stay to eat dinner with our bunk?"

"Why of course, girls," Dad replied, and Mom agreed.

Mrs. Miller escorted our parents to the office, where they would wait for us to finish our meal.

Jay ran up ahead to the mess hall doors.

"Jay, no, wait," I said urgently.

"What is it, Lex?" Jay asked.

I walked toward Jay as she stood by the door and tugged at her arm, linking it with mine. "Come with me," I said adamantly.

"But, I want to hang out with Danny," Jay insisted.

"You will, this will only take a minute. Follow me."

I led Jay behind the mess hall to a plot of grass. I took out the two scrolls secured in my pocket.

"Aren't you curious?" I asked.

Jay looked at me and said, "Our star maps. What should we do with them?"

"Let's open them up," I replied.

Jay took the scrolls out of my hands and looked at them. "I have no idea what this means. What's that sound?" Jay asked.

We sat there quietly and listened. A nearby plant rustled, but there was no wind.

"Izzy on Earth! Izzy on Earth!" Izzy screamed as he jumped out from the plant.

CHAPTER 38

JAYCEE

"Izzy!" I shouted as I ran over to my favorite little friend. "How are you here? What happened? Does Artie know?"

I was so excited I could barely catch my breath. Nabu jumped out from my pocket and onto Izzy's head.

"Well, how else do you think this little guy made it here?" Izzy asked.

"Izzy on Earth!" Nabu smiled and laughed.

Lex was not amused. I don't think she was convinced that this was true. "Artie is going to be so upset. You guys should not be here," she said.

"Well, Izzy is here, and I'm happy about it," I said as I rubbed Izzy's tummy.

He giggled and jumped up onto Lex. "Don't be upset, Lex. Artie knows and he'll be DIPping in. Besides, I'm here to help. What do you have there?" he asked, pointing to the star maps.

Lex couldn't help but smile at Izzy. "Oh, those are our star maps. We don't know how to read them."

"Well ... let me take a look. I've seen a star map or two in my day," Izzy said.

Izzy plopped down on the grass and opened the maps. "Aha ... yes ... this makes sense," he said.

Nabu jumped on the map and looked on with Izzy.

"What do you see, Izzy?" I asked.

"Well, it seems there is a message for you to uncover here on Earth. I can't grasp the exact message, but it seems like you've already seen it before," Izzy said as he wrapped up the maps.

"Wait, that's it? You're done? What's the message?" I asked.

"Jay, I don't know. Maybe you can tell me. You are the one that has the power of keen sight," Izzy said.

"Harold is here," Lex said.

"Of course he is, perfect timing," I said.

Izzy and Nabu sat on my lap as Lex turned to talk to Harold. Good thing we were alone and there were no campers around. They would have seen me petting the air above my own lap and Lex talking out loud to her left side. It would be quite an embarrassing sight.

ALEXA

I was getting frustrated. "Harold, this is no time for guessing games. We are supposed to be having dinner with our bunk. What is it?" I asked him.

Harold pointed up to the sky. It frustrated me when he didn't answer me. What did that mean? I looked up at the sky. I didn't see anything. "Harold, can you be clearer?" I asked.

Harold floated over to Jay. "Jay, you've seen the message in the sky," I translated.

"Lex, what is he talking about?" Jay asked.

I repeated Harold's message again slowly: "You've seen the message in the sky." I thought really hard. "I've got it, the planetarium. Jay, we have to go back to the telescope!"

CHAPTER 39

JAYCEE

We ran up the hill toward the planetarium. Harold, Nabu, and Izzy were by our side. It was dark, all the lights were off.

"Oh no, it's closed," I said. I turned the knob. "It's locked!" I screamed out to Lex.

Lex was huffing and puffing her way up the hill. "What should we do? We have to get in there before someone sees us," Lex said frantically.

Izzy bounced up to the door and attempted to push it open.

"Izzy, I think you're too small," I said.

"Oh really? Well I'd like you to stand back. Izzy on Earth! Izzy is here for a reason," he stated, determined.

His fuzzy coat fluffed up, and his shiny blue shimmer glowed brightly. The energy around our little blue friend started expanding out toward the door.

"Keep doing that, Izzy. Look, the doors are rattling!" I shouted.

Izzy closed his eyes and concentrated harder. His shimmer was directed toward the door. The door lit up bright blue, and before we knew it, Bang. It flew open.

"You've got to teach me how to do that," I said to Izzy.

We walked in. Lex ran over to the wall and switched on the lights. "We need to move fast, Harold says," Lex directed.

From a distance we could hear Celeste calling out our names. "Alexa, Jaycee, where are you now?"

"Jay, are you in here?" Danny called out.

"Danny's here," I said to Lex. "Should we open the door?"

"No, Celeste is with him. Let's just do this quickly and then we can let them in," Lex instructed. Lex put out her hand. "Izzy, the star maps please?"

Izzy gave Lex the star maps, and I led us over to the telescopes. "Okay let's take a look," I said.

Lex opened up the maps and spread them out on the floor in front of us. "Jay, quick, look through the scope," Lex said impatiently.

I gently focused and looked through the eyepiece. "I don't see anything," I said.

"Harold says you need to concentrate," Lex said. "Let your eyes adjust to the light."

The stars were bright and started to dance once again. Their light went in and out and up and down, trying to connect to each other.

"Something's happening," I said.

Nabu jumped onto my shoulder and Izzy climbed up my leg. The stars were trying to form a message. They were dancing around each other trying to find their rhythm.

"Okay, I see a G and an R."

"What else? Is there a message?" Lex asked.

I hear footsteps outside.

"Girls? Girls are you in there?" Celeste knocked on the door.

"Oh no! Quick, what else does it say?" Lex asked.

"G. R. E. E. N," I spelled out.

"Green? That's it?" Lex asked.

"Izzy loves Green!" Izzy said with a smile. His skin shimmer changed to the color green.

Nabu saw this and quickly did the same. "Nabu green," Nabu said.

"Wait, what's that?" I asked.

The star maps were lighting up.

"Jay? Are you in there?" Celeste repeated.

"I saw them go this way. We'll find them," Danny said from behind the door.

"Let's go around the back entrance," we heard Celeste answer.

"I really want Danny to see this too. He already saw Nabu. What's the big deal?" I asked.

Lex shook her head no.

Izzy quickly bounced over to the back door and locked it shut. "Izzy loves green and wants to know more," he said.

"Green, what do we know about the color green?" I asked. The star maps continued to light up and glow.

"Look, they're forming an outline," I said.

The glow from the stars shone on the maps. An image appeared before us. "It looks like a person," Lex said.

"It's an outline of us," I asserted.

Purple shone out from the center of our heads, and a faint green light radiated from the center of our chests.

"Power-points," I said to Lex.

"I think so too," she agreed.

The door started to rattle open. "Quick Lex, grab the maps," I whispered to her.

"Alexa? Jaycee?" Celeste called out.

Izzy bounced over to us with his green shimmer shining brightly. "Green. Green. Green."

On his last bounce, as his feet touched the maps, his energy ignited a big green blast. "Uh-oh," Izzy said as he was thrown back by the force of his own energy.

His shimmer ignited a huge burst of green flames. They leapt out from the maps and filled the room.

"Izzy! What did you do?" I screamed.

The green blast ignited the star maps into a big green fireball. We all jumped back.

The star maps disintegrated right in front of us.

"They're gone!" Lex yelled, panicking.

"We need those maps, Izzy, what did you do?!" I shouted.

Nabu redirected our attention to the fire. He jumped on my shoulder, and Izzy held on tight to Lex.

"Fire! Fire!" Nabu shrieked.

The green flames rapidly moved toward us.

"I didn't realize that would happen, I'm sorry," Izzy said nervously.

"Quick, get some water, we need to put this fire out!" I hollered.

"Jay? Is that you? I just heard her. They're in here," Danny said to Celeste from behind the rear door.

144

"Hold on, I have a key," we heard Celeste say.

Green fire started to surround the room. "It's hot, and I'm scared," Lex said.

"Is this real?" I asked.

"It sure looks real to me. Quick, find some water, Anything!" Lex instructed.

"I think we should just *ment* it away," Izzy says.

"Izzy you can't do that here. It's Earth remember?" I said.

The door opened.

"Girls?" Celeste asked.

Celeste and Danny entered the burning room.

"Oh my goodness!" Celeste said, as she took in the scene.

The fire was real. Celeste ran over to the wall and grabbed the extinguisher. She yanked on the lever and blew the white foam onto the green flames.

The flames died quickly, and Lex looked relieved, though still quite alarmed. Izzy clung onto Lex's arm tightly. Nabu wrapped himself around my head like a hat. Celeste and Danny stood in front of us wide-eyed in shock.

I looked to Lex. She looked to me. We both turned to them. We were speechless. The room was silent.

"Well, this is awkward," Izzy said.

Celeste gasped. Her eyes widened more. Did she just hear Izzy? Celeste slowly took a step toward us. I looked to Lex. Lex looked just as surprised.

Celeste carefully spoke, still unsure of what just happened. "Green fire. A little blue koala bear that talks, a short stocky man who looks like Santa Claus, and a monkey. At least I think it's a monkey anyway. Do one of you want to explain this to me?" Celeste asked.

Lex and I gasped. I looked to Lex. She looked at me and smiled widely.

"I knew it all along," Lex said.

"Maybe we should all sit down. You see, we've had a bit of an adventure, and it all started with a little pink man," I said with a smile.

REFERENCES

We would like to acknowledge the following resources:

"A little birdie in a tree," Softball Practice Plan, online at
http://www.softballpracticeplan.com/softball-cheers-chants-songs/.
Accessed 2 February 2015. (i, ii)

"Announcement Song," Ultimate Camp Resource, online at
http://www.ultimatecampresource.com/site/camp-activity/announcement-song.html.
Accessed 2 February 2015. (iii)

"A-W-E-S-O-M-E," Ultimate Camp Resource, online at
http://www.ultimatecampresource.com/site/camp-activity/a-w-e-s-o-m-e.html.
Accessed 2 February 2015. (iv, v)

ACKNOWLEDGMENTS

Gwen, thanks for your assistance editing this book.

Jason, you helped us find solutions when we needed them.

Sylvie, you're a blessing in our lives.

Lexie, we appreciate your support and treasure your friendship.

Star Seeds, your feedback was greatly valued and inspirational to us.

Esther, we couldn't have done this book without you. Thank you for the butterfly.

ABOUT THE AUTHORS
Heather & Samara Silverman

Samara   Heather

This book is coauthored by Heather and Samara Silverman. They refer to themselves as "twin sisters" but are actually part of a set of triplets.

Although vastly different in appearance and personalities, the two are inseparable and each other's best friend.

Heather is a filmmaker, and Samara is an attorney.

For more information on Forever SoulSisters visit **www.foreversoulsisters.com.**

Made in the USA
Middletown, DE
12 February 2021